MW00877353

Having The Dinosaur's Baby

A Pregnancy Of Convenience Romance

A complete story, brought to you by best selling paranormal romance author Jane Rowe.

The good news: curvy Jean has finally found a handsome and powerful man who is ready to have her baby... he goes by the name of Vel.

The bad news: Vel is a Velociraptor shifter from a mysterious island, one which her and her paleontologist friends have crash landed their boat on.

Now stuck on a dangerous island with all the other dinosaur shifters seeing humans as nothing more than food, Jean must carry the scent of a dinosaur to make it across the island to safety.

The only reliable way to do that?

To have a dinosaur shifter baby growing inside her belly.

And if that means she has to be Vel's mate in order to ensure she survives, so be it!

But with her new baby growing at an accelerated rate and the baby father's friends all trying to eat her, can Jean stay alive long enough to enjoy her new family life?

Find out in this hot and exciting new kind of shifter romance, brought to you by best selling author Jane Rowe.

Suitable for over 18s only due to hot sex scenes only conceivable in the Jurassic world.

Tip: Search **Shifter Club** on Amazon to see more of our great books.

Get Free Romance eBooks!

Hi there. As a special thank you for buying this book, for a limited time I want to send you some great ebooks completely **free of charge** directly to your email! You can get it by going to this page:

www.saucyromancebooks.com/physical

You can see a the cover of these books on the next page:

These ebooks are so exclusive you can't even buy them. When you download them I'll also send you updates when new books like this are available.

Again, that link is:

www.saucyromancebooks.com/physical

ISBN-13: 978-1517394417

ISBN-10: 1517394414

Contents

Chapter 1

Jean Moncrieff had always dreamed that one day she could become a great explorer, very much in keeping with Darwin, a scientist and scholar after her own heart. Now, as she set forth with her graduating class of fellow paleontologists in hopes of breaking new ground in their field, she couldn't help but indulge herself in a girlish bout of excitement.

The group had decided to go big for their final thesis and search for signs of super-continents that might have predated Pangaea, the single continent which had begun to break up right about the same time that the big boys had come out to play. Dinosaurs! And what Jean wouldn't have given just to have been able to see them in all their huge, majestic glory. From a safe distance, of course.

Well, doubtless that was ever going to happen, but at least she hoped to find a few traces of them off the shores of Bermuda. Bermuda, which was somewhere off the coast of Florida, was just one point in three, including another point at Puerto Rico and a third at Miami, which encompassed the infamous Bermuda Triangle so popular in urban myth. Although she didn't believe most of what they said about the area's penchant to steal airplanes from the sky and suck ships right down into the water, Jean did believe there was definitely something of interest there.

Measurements taken in that vicinity by the computer program back at Berkeley had predicted the place was once part of the shoreline of Pangaea, not to mention it was highly probable it had been part of a previous continent even before that. Now it was a deep-sea coral bed, and Bermuda itself arose from it as several small islands that were all interconnected beneath the waves. Fossil evidence found there, and indeed the predominant array of different types of current crustaceans in the area, indicated that the little hotbed had a great deal to tell about the past, and her team was eager to learn its secrets.

"Captain? How long do you think it's going to take to get to the island in this little scow?" asked Amanda Picket in a bored voice from her vantage closer to him. The captain had been hired specifically to take the ten scientists to the main island, where a much larger boat meant for surveying the ocean depths was waiting to take them out to sea.

"Don't worry your pretty head about that, little missy," he told her in his slight southern drawl. "I'll get everyone there in one piece."

"So you've never had any trouble with going through the triangle in all your years of sailing?" Jean clarified with a little smirk. "I would imagine you know better than to believe in such stuff since you deal with this area every single day."

"That's not a thing to talk about while we're out on the water, little girl," he admonished her. "You don't wanna call any bad luck our way, do you?"

"No, of course not, sir," said Jean nervously. Was he serious about that? She certainly hoped not. She wasn't especially superstitious as a general rule, but this *was* the Bermuda triangle, after all. With so many stories out there, it was difficult to believe there wasn't something unusual about the place. So far, however, the water didn't look any different from any other ocean she'd seen in the course of her twenty-six years.

"Superstitious nonsense," she told herself under her breath, and Captain Luke Claiborne's brow shot up mockingly. "Isn't it?" she added nervously.

"Oh, now, I wouldn't go believing that completely," he said. "I've never had any troubles myself, but there's plenty of my friends who've had a close call over the years. Usually it happens thanks to bad weather, but still, you never can tell what might be out there, right?"

"Right," Jean answered uncertainly. Was he just trying to scare her, or was he being serious? It was difficult to tell.

"In fact, there's supposed to be a storm coming in later tonight," Claiborne added with a wicked grin that gave her the answer. He was messing with her big time. "My goodness, Miss Moncrieff, you've got lovely, deep green eyes, haven't you? I suppose I didn't realize it until they were open so very wide. But never mind, I'll pilot this boat safely to your destination. I've never failed to do so yet, and I'm not about to start now."

"That's good to hear, Captain," she told him. "I really don't think I'd like to end up at the bottom of the ocean if it can be avoided."

"I couldn't agree with you more, my dear," he chuckled. "Why don't you find a chair and catch some sun while you still can?

That storm's supposed to come in within the next two or three hours, and we'll all have to go below to wait it out."

"Thank you for letting me know, Captain," Jean replied. "But, I think I'll head down there right now. I still have a few more chapters to read before I finish that novel anyway."

"Too bad," he smirked. "I was looking forward to the view."

"Behave yourself, Captain," she admonished him. "I've got bigger fish to fry on this voyage than an old salt like you."

"I'm not nearly old enough to ignore a little beauty like you," he called after her as he watched her go. Jean stepped down the ladder and headed for the little door that led into the women's quarters, flopping down on the smallish mattress that served as a bed for the three day voyage. Her book was still waiting for her on her pillow, and she settled down to read it with a satisfied sigh.

The other five women returned to the hold shortly after the ship began to rock violently, causing Jean to lose her place in her book. "Dammit," she grumbled. "Has the storm begun, then?"

"Yes," Tabitha Gray told her nervously. "I've never seen anything like it, really. I believe the lightning was striking sideways. Must be the difference in the magnetic pull around here or something.

"That fits well with everything we've heard about the area," Jean agreed. "If any of it is to be believed, of course."

"Well I gotta tell you, I'm feeling a pretty strong sense of belief right this minute," Amanda said as she laid back on her own bed. "The whole world seems like it's spinning from here, don't you think?"

"If you're going to get sick, find the bucket," Jean told her as she thumbed through her book for her page so she could at least mark the thing. "I don't think anyone is going to want to wade through human waste while we're being tossed all around the cabin."

"Do you think the men are doing any better?" Tabitha smirked.

"Doubtful," Jean said with a shrug. "You know those four are all weak-minded fools. They'll be blubbering in their beer before the night is over."

"Always the cynical one, Jean," said the captain from the doorway. "I was just making sure you ladies have everything you need? I'll have to remain above to steer throughout the night. I don't want this boat to end up at the wrong place when all this is done. So, you'll be pretty much on your own if you don't ask me for anything while I'm here now."

"Do you really think it's that bad?" Jean asked worriedly.

"I've never seen anything quite like this storm," he replied. "I'm going to have to lash myself to the wheel just to stay aboard."

"Is that true?" she gasped.

"The compass has gone completely haywire, and I can't get the radio to function at all," he said. "I have nothing to go by but the stars, and there's no way I'm going to see any of those in that cloud-filled sky," he said. "There's no knowing what will happen at this point. So maybe all these legends of the Bermuda triangle could be true after all, eh?"

"You're not helping to calm anyone in this room down, Captain," Jean admonished him. "Why don't you get back up there and do your job? If we really need anything, I'm sure we could fend for ourselves."

With a cagey grin and an exaggerated salute, Captain Claiborne headed quickly up the stairs. At the top, he opened the little door, and Jean could see the wind and waves whipping madly about beneath a sky full of lightning. Her brow furrowed as she closed the door and returned to her bunk again. He was right about one thing. She'd never seen anything like that before either.

*****

Jean had been wide awake and ready for anything when the boat impacted with the rocks. It didn't take a scientist to figure out they must have found land of some sort, but being a scientist surely made it easier to keep her panic in check and lead everyone from the two rooms in the hold safely out onto the deck.

The Captain was nowhere to be seen, unfortunately, and a closer examination of the wheel revealed a most alarming reason. Instead of the longer rope she'd expected to find him connected to, only a shorter remnant remained. It looked as though it had been literally ripped apart, and the Captain had been detached and forcibly taken out to a watery grave.

"Dammit," Jean grumbled as she looked at the boat. "We won't be going anywhere in this ship without some major repairs. All of you, we've got to get out of this boat and find shelter somewhere on this island until the storm passes. We can't risk being dragged back out to sea. Somebody weight the anchor, maybe it will hold so we can come back for our supplies when it's safe."

"Since when are you in charge here?" asked Brad with a sneer. "You know that I'm the team leader."

"Well then, Brad, by all means start leading."

"Everyone do what Jean said for now," he conceded. "We'll worry about stoking my overactive ego later on."

"Aye, aye, sir!" the others saluted, and then they all dove off the boat and waded further up the beach to a more accessible shore. Climbing the face of a huge cliff had not appealed to them. Trekking through the shallows right in the middle of a hazardous lightning storm was pretty nerve-racking to say the least, but they all made it to the shore and headed for the higher cliffs via a small path instead.

"We totally need to find a cave," said Brad once they were at the top. "Head for that higher rise and make for the hilltop. If there's any sort of a cave at all, it would have to be there somewhere."

The rain was beating down on everyone so hard that consideration went right out the window. The faster members went ahead, figuring they could find the cave and lead in the others when they finally arrived. Jean herself was neither among the first nor the last, but having a bit of sense she realized the mud in the dirty area would hinder any attempts to walk, and thus headed for the edge of the trees in search of a slightly firmer path.

Once there, however, she realized that from here she wouldn't be able to see the progress of her peers. She contemplated whether or not she wanted to be out of their sights as well, and was about to head back out to the edge with them when suddenly an arm snaked around her belly from behind.

"Well, well, if it isn't the little optimist," said Captain Claiborne as he drew her against him. "Leave it to you to look for another way."

"You're alive?" she gasped, preventing his wet, muddy hands from moving up or down her body as he buried his nose against her neck. She shoved herself away from him and landed with a splat on her backside. "Gross!"

"Hey, I'm not that bad, am I?" he complained when he heard that.

"Not you, you dirty old salt, this mud," she explained as he moved toward her with an extended hand. Rather than take it, though, Jean looked strangely at a creature that was struggling in the mire as well. "Hey, what is this? There's no way I'm looking at you. You shouldn't even exist."

"What are you talking about?" asked Claiborne as he helped her up at the same time she picked up the fox-sized lizard.

"This animal went extinct a very, very long time ago," she explained.

"How do you know that?" he wanted to know as he took it from her hands.

"Well, I did just get an A on a test about it," she shrugged. "There's no way that thing is a new species. It looks just like some sort of a cynodontian."

"Whatever that is," he shrugged.

"This thing is considered an ancestor to today's mammals," she told him. "This island must be some sort of a throwback to the pre-historic past. And if this guy is here, there could very well be other types of pre-historic flora and fauna present as well."

"Is any of this discussion going to lead to me taking you off to some cave by ourselves and getting me laid?" he asked her then.

"Oh!" Jean gasped. "I am not going to have sex with you!"

"Are you sure?" he asked, brow raised and lips pursed. "There's no telling how long we'll be trapped on Pangaea Island."

"What did you call it?" she asked with a shocked expression.

"I've heard of a place like this," he shrugged. "That's what the other captains call it. I figure this must be that island considering this lizard thing—"

While Captain Claiborne was still talking, the ground began to shake. But it wasn't an earthquake, since the shaking seemed to come in a pattern, like footfalls of something really big.

"Not to interrupt, Captain, but don't you hear that?"

"Hear what?" he paused, pricking his ears to listen as well. "That doesn't sound like somebody we'd like to meet. I think we'd better get to a cave quick."

"You mean—"

"I mean *run!*"

Jean didn't take any more time to give his words thought. Her heart began to pound as the sound of the steps drew closer, and she started to run. However, not too many steps later her feet snagged in some brush, and she toppled down into a small ditch. The call of a Tyrannosaurus Rex sounded remarkably like an amplified monitor lizard on steroids. This one in particular stepped right past her as it continued on after her recent companion. Soon after, she heard him scream.

She wondered if this time he was dead for sure, or if he had yet again managed to survive.

*****

Just because the dinosaur had gone past her didn't mean that Jean was any safer than the captain had been. She was hardly foolish enough to think it wouldn't double back if it sensed movement anytime soon. However, the pouring rain and extreme winds were making her little ditch into a raucous swimming pool that was so deep she would have to keep swimming in it if she wanted to remain.

Not to mention, she had just come to the conclusion that she was floating around inside of a huge footprint, which didn't make her feel any better. If there was a footprint along the same path the beast had just traveled, that meant surely he would come this way again sometime. She really wanted to get out of there before another one came along while they were at it.

She was feeling completely exhausted by the time help arrived as a pair of legs that suddenly appeared at her eye level on the fallen tree which had been hiding her from view. She thought at first that one of her team had come looking for her. Probably Brad since he was the bravest despite being so annoying. However, when her eyes traced upward, she knew that she was dead wrong.

The eyes that stared down at her were strange, almost a shade of gold. And the chiseled features of the man who owned them looked more Cro-Magnon than she liked. The fact that the guy was holding a long, wooden spear didn't instill any confidence in her either. Could anybody really blame her when she let out a loud, piercing scream as she attempted to swim away from him?

"No yell!" the man insisted as he jumped down into the pool with her, quickly stopping her attempts at departure as he pulled her flush to him and covered her mouth with one hand while he dragged her out with the other. "We leave here now! Not safe!"

"You can talk?" she gasped against his hand, then remembered that with her mouth covered that meant that she, herself, could not.

"Stay quiet," he said softly. "Follow."

"Y-yes," she said softly as she fell into step behind him. Not surprisingly, he took her toward the mountain and as soon as they broke free of the forest, he grabbed her hand and broke into a run. Jean almost stumbled again, and the man did not hesitate to throw her over his shoulder and move on. Jean didn't even have the strength to protest, so she simply slumped against him and let him have his way. She figured she must have lost consciousness when they were suddenly entering a cave in the side of the mountain.

Inside a huge main cave, several large hearths dominated, with many people gathered around them. What looked like a shaman with the horn of a triceratops on his hat danced around in front of them, telling some sort of story that was mostly rendered with sounds and movements rather than an actual language.

Although intrigued, Jean was just too exhausted to pay much attention, and the man carrying her did not bother to stop, but continued on further into the cave. Finally, he entered the opening to a side cave in which a much smaller hearth fire burned. Nearby, a pile of furs dominated a small space, and that was where he laid her down.

"What is this place?" she wanted to know.

"Shh!" he hissed as he touched her lips. "Rest. Head hurt. Need sleep."

He touched the side of Jean's head, and his fingers came away with a bit of blood, which he showed to her. When she started with alarm, and would have sat up, he stopped her. "Rest now. I get Trip. He heal you."

Jean nodded then, understanding what was making movement seem so difficult. She must have a concussion, and she'd probably lost a great deal of blood, too. She hoped this Trip person, who was probably that shaman she had seen before, would be able to treat the wound and prevent it from getting infected.

"Who are you?" she asked the man softly before he moved away, her fingers reaching out to catch at his arm.

He looked down at her hand, then cast her a rather sensual stare as he said, "Vel. My mother calls me that. You like her. You human."

Jean cast him a strange look when he said that. "I'm human, yes. But if you're not human, then what are you?"

"Vel," he repeated with a smirk. Then he stood up, and suddenly transformed into a very real, very frightening-looking velociraptor.

"No fucking way!" Jean shrieked, and she passed out from the shock. Vel immediately changed back again.

"Maybe not show?" he said with a shrug. He turned and headed out of his cave again, catching the old one's eye. Trip had seen him enter the cave as he told his tale, and so he had finished up and was now waiting for his return. The conversation they had was mostly done in gestures and grunts, but they understood it to mean this:

"I've found a mate, keeper," said Vel. "She evaded the largest ones, but she is injured. Will you come to heal her?"

"You know that she is not one of us," said the keeper with a stubborn frown. "I could smell the stench of her frail humanity from here. She won't last a week in this place. Why bother to save her now?"

"My mother lasted far longer than a week, grand keeper of the years," Vel insisted. "If you will not save her, then perhaps she will."

"No woman shall usurp my rights from me," the old man growled. "I am Trip, and I am at one with the spirits. What magic could your mother work that I cannot?"

"I do not know, old master," Vel said. "I only know the memories say there's much we could learn from this girl. But if I do not take her to mate, she cannot possibly survive to tell us anything at all. If her smell is so obvious to you, it will be noted by others as well. You know this to be true."

"Very well, then, for the sake of history, I shall allow her to live," the old one sighed. Then, his horns slid back into his skull so that he looked very much like a Neanderthal. Vel smiled as he allowed the man to step past and precede him into his cave. The girl remained still among his furs.

Chapter 2

"Biggest injury is on her head," Trip signed and grunted to Vel. "I will have to use the bone needle to tie the wound shut. Lucky for you, I have brought it along."

Vel simply nodded in response. He knew that the old one would use magic drink to cause the girl to rest before he used the bone, but that meant they would need to wake her so she could swallow the potion. He let her rest until the old man had finished chewing up the roots and begun to smile crazily and sway about as he spit the stuff into hot water.

"It needs sweetening," Vel signed decisively.

"You wish to spoil her already?" the old man scoffed. But he produced another potion and added it to the first. "This ought to do the trick. Sit her up, so we can get her to drink."

"As you wish, master."

When Jean felt someone shaking her awake, she thought at first that she was back at college and had overslept, and her roommate had come to rouse her. "I'm up, I'm up," she muttered as she tried to sit up. Then she realized the supportive hands on her back and on her shoulder were much larger than Shannon's hands could possibly be.

She opened her eyes and saw that she was in a cave with two strange men, and she screamed. She slapped at Vel's hands as she tried to scramble away from him, but he held her fast so she wouldn't injure herself further in her attempts.

"Let me go!" she gasped as she clawed at his hands, but Vel refused to do it, and eventually she began to calm down. She slumped against him, breathing heavily, and Vel used one of his hands to smooth her hair away from her face.

"Drink," he said in his most soothing tone. "Drink all."

The old Neanderthal stepped forward with a ceramic bowl-shaped item that was filled with a steaming brew of some sort. "Trip help," he told her.

Even though Jean knew it was probably some primitive form of medicine she did not refuse. If the medicine man thought she needed medicine, she reasoned, that must be because she did. Besides, wasn't all of this a hallucination anyway? She must be aboard the boat and dreaming the whole thing, so cooperating with this guy surely wasn't going to hurt.

The drink was bitter and sweet at the same time, but she managed to swallow it all. Then she realized that the younger man was still holding her in his arms. Calmer now, she was more in control of her responses, and he could tell, so when she asked him again to let go, this time he did it.

She saw the medicine man threading something through a hole in a bone, and she grimaced and shook her head. Feeling around, she discovered that her field medical kit was still in her breast pocket, where she'd placed it before they'd waded ashore. When she pulled it out, the old man stared with fascination as she pulled out the suture kit that was packed inside.

Motioning with his hands, he let her know he'd like to see what she was holding. Jean made motions that she hoped would explain to him what to do, both with the sutures and with the scissors to cut them after they were tied off.

When he took the suture she was showing him, it accidentally pierced his thumb, and he stared in amazement, making her giggle. She felt a bit of blood gush out of the cut on the side of her head, and she instinctively shot up a hand to put pressure on it.

Knowing he wanted to stitch the wound, Jean laid on her side on the fur and moved her hand out of the way, casting the old man a stoic glance of invitation. Using about ten of the sutures, the shaman made short work of his task. All the while he did it, Jean wondered where a Neanderthal would have learned to sew shut a wound to begin with. If this world really had been cut off from everyone for millions of years, and they couldn't possibly have come up with the idea independently, that had to mean they'd had contact with others in recent times.

And yet they remained here, firmly rooted in the distant past. They had clearly adapted the ability to shift forms as a way to survive, however strange the prospect might seem.

All such thoughts immediately vacated her mind once the old man moved away and the younger one returned to her side. He seemed rather possessive to Jean as he gently ran his hand over the prickly stitches, and then drew her against his side as he bowed slightly to Trip.

"Thank you," said Jean softly, and the old man dropped his eyes as he left. Confused by the reaction, she glanced at Vel uncertainly.

"Females," he said, fumbling to find the words. "Only talk to other females or their mate."

"I see," Jean said, one brow raised. "Well, I'm not going to fail to be polite over some silly custom you've obviously come up with to subjugate your ladies. If the man has helped me, I was taught to express my gratitude. It's the right thing to do."

"Bad idea to stand out," Vel replied. "Much safer to fit in."

"I don't want to fit in," Jean scoffed. "I just want to get off this island and back to where I belong. Unfortunately, I don't think the boat's in any shape to sail until we figure out how to fix the hole in the hull."

"You have ship?"

"How are you even able to talk in the first place?" Jean asked him then. "Who taught you to speak English? Have other people been here before this?"

"My mother," he explained. "She came on ship. Jerris eat all but her. Jerris eat all outsiders who come here. Not want them to come, not want them to go again if they do."

"Jerris? You mean that Tyrannosaurus-Rex I narrowly escaped?"

"Not know your big word, but Jerris one who chase you into pit," he said. "Others chase you like Jerris unless we cover your scent."

Smirking then, he pulled Jean closer and rubbed his bared chest on her back.

"What are you doing?" she gasped, moving away.

Grinning, Vel caught her again and turned her around, rubbing the front of her against him as well. "Cover scent," he said, rubbing his arms down hers and then grasping her hips, bringing their bodies flush against each other. "Sex even better way to cover scent."

"Wh-what?" she gaped up at him. "You want to have sex? Right here, right now, just so I smell right?"

"Mate with me," he nodded, still holding her close.

"No!" she complained, trying unsuccessfully to push free of his embrace. "I don't even know you!"

"Then get my scent," he shrugged. "You like. Make good mate."

"Excuse me? Where I come from, the decision to have sex isn't based solely on the scent of the prospective mate," Jean began to lecture. As she spoke, Vel kept smelling her—along the throat, up and over her ear, back down to her neck, then down into the valley between her breasts. When he did that last, Jean gasped with shock, both because he'd done such a thing at all, and because what he was doing was really making her hot.

"Scent, touch, taste?" he murmured, then ran his tongue lightly over the spot he'd just been smelling before rubbing his rough, stubbly cheek there as well. Which was when Jean realized that he must have some idea how to cut his hair as well as remove hair from his face, too. Did they have razors? Or some other sharp object? Or maybe they'd made tools out of dinosaurs' teeth? Her curiosity was piqued in an instant.

Jean's wandering, ever-curious mind came back to reality with a snap when she realized that Vel's current quest had not ended. He pulled at her shirt, and when he couldn't figure out what to do about the buttons he simply yanked, making them all pop off. She sucked in a shocked breath.

"Stop that!" she protested. "What am I supposed to wear now, thanks to you? I can see you're feeling kind of frisky here, but I really think you ought to cool your jets."

"Cool what?" he asked huskily. He stood up fully and leaned in to kiss her lips instead. "Jets?"

"Flying ships," Jean explained, though he barely gave her time to say the words past his kisses. "Now come on, stop it. My head's still really painful, and I think that drink is hitting me hard now. I'm feeling really dizzy."

Vel backed off and tilted her head back a bit so he could look into her eyes. "Not all better. Get rest. We mate after."

"I did not say I was going to mate with you!' Jean protested, making him puff out his cheeks with amusement. This made her laugh.

"My mother make that sound too," he said. "It called 'laugh', yes? I never do right."

"You don't know how to laugh?" Jean asked with a shocked expression. "You can shave off your beard somehow, and your people can use a needle and sinew to sew up wounds and make leather clothing, but you can't figure out how to laugh? This place really is weird."

"Those skills sacred. Known only by few," he shrugged, and ran his fingers curiously over top of the stitching at her jawline, looking at them with fascination. "Afraid I might hurt."

"Well, it does hurt, I suppose," she conceded. "But it helps, too. And anyone can learn how to do it, not just the ones with the help of the gods or whatever. I could show you how to sew without incurring any sort of wrath at all." When she saw Vel cringe at these words she couldn't help but smile. "Laugh with me, Vel."

Jean laughed again, and Vel tried to mimic her. He came close, but he didn't have the amusement right. Maybe he wasn't fully aware of the reason a person laughed to begin with, or maybe he wasn't amused enough himself. Either way, his lack of skill had her laughing harder than ever, and finally he got it right.

"You good teacher," he said. "Before, I know to feel happy, but my people hide feelings. When you laugh, I got to laugh too. Just comes out."

"Well, I'm glad to be of service, then," Jean smirked. "Maybe I'll show you how to sew sometime while I'm at it."

"Get rest," he said then, pressing her back onto the furs and following her there, dragging her into his arms to keep her close. "Not try to leave. Too dangerous without me."

"You think so?" she scoffed, remembering full well that there was a crazy, huge and hungry carnivorous tyrannosaur just waiting for her to step outside the caves again. She wasn't stupid enough to think she could outrun the thing with her head in such sad shape. She was just going to have to humor Vel the shape shifting Velociraptor until she was feeling better.

Besides, he really was kind of cute. At least it wasn't going to be a chore.

*****

Jean opened her eyes again after what felt like many hours later. Being inside a dark cave, it was impossible to know how many, but the fire in the hearth had died down to the point that it was little more than coals. Next to the hearth she could see two things that might be helpful. One was a large bowl made of wood that smelled like it was used for waste. The other was a large pile of burnables like wood, plants, and dried dung.

She slid free of Vel's arms and went over to the bowl, relieving herself. Afterwards, she grabbed some of the burnables and threw them onto the fire. Before she had completed this second task, she felt a kiss on the top of her head, followed by Vel's strong arms encircling her again.

"Get plenty of scent on you, then go eat with others," he told her. "Introduce you to tribe. No talk to males. Not safe. Should mate before we go."

"I already told you I'm not going to do that," Jean grumbled, although the rather large erection he was currently rubbing against her buttocks was seriously giving her some second thoughts on that decision.

"Safer," he coaxed, rubbing some more. "We make new life, nobody try to eat you."

"What?" she gasped, pushing out of his arms to face him more fully. "You want to make a baby just so nobody tries to eat me? Oh my God, I can't even begin to process this!"

Taking a deep, steadying breath, Jean began to pace back and forth in front of him. She wanted desperately to just run away and find out if anybody had started to repair their ship. She wanted to get far away from this totally hot, totally primitive man as fast as her legs could carry her. She wanted to—but she knew that she couldn't. Even uninjured, she would never be able to survive the attempt.

"Listen, I think you're getting ideas about us that you really shouldn't be having," she told him then. "See, I'm not staying here forever. I have a life back in the real world. I'm supposed to be studying dinosaurs as creatures from the past, not living in some cave with them and birthing their babies."

Vel smirked. "Not real dinosaur. Just sometimes. They are food, I am hunter for tribe. Become dinosaur just to get food. That all."

"You guys learned to become dinosaurs just so you could hunt for food, huh?" she asked, fascinated in spite of herself. "So that would have been an interesting thing to see, how humans would have been able to develop the ability to shift like that. Maybe it's some sort of selection process over time, bred into the shifters so they could specialize—"

"The gods give us ability. Choose us when born," he shrugged. "Like Trip, he healer because chosen, in here he horned one, but when he joined hunt was like Jerris—very big. And Jerris protect this place because chosen. I feed the people because chosen, and decided to be like father in form to do it. See?"

"Yeah, I get it," she nodded. "But that's just so—I can't believe you can shift like that. It's physically impossible, isn't it? I mean—so you're telling me that this Jerris is also a shifter? That he can shrink down to the size of a man or balloon up into a huge monster? How is that even possible? Where would the excess matter be stored when he wasn't using it? It's just too amazing to be real—"

"We mate first," he said decisively as he dragged Jean back into his arms. He gave her no time to protest again before he slid his tongue between her lips. She hesitated only a moment before she found her own tongue meeting his in a searingly hot kiss that took her breath away. Her heart pounded hard in her chest, and he rested a hand over it, letting her know that he was aware.

Jean's hands trembled as they rested on Vel's hips as he continued to kiss her. She was certain other parts of her were trembling as well, especially her legs. Her knees had become like jelly and holding him was the only way she could find to keep from falling. His hands came up to fondle her breasts as he pressed his magnificent erection against her belly, making her gasp.

"No, Vel, stop," she said weakly.

"Not smell like you want me to stop," he smirked sensuously against her lips as he took a whiff of the air. "Smell very ready."

Blushing at this rather true observation, Jean nevertheless pressed Vel away from her and shook her head. "It's a bad idea. As you said, sex leads to babies, and that's the last thing I'm going to want to do is get pregnant while I'm out doing field work. Especially with a child that would probably become a shape shifter as well. I mean, how would the kid function in modern America if it started turning into a dinosaur and terrorizing the neighborhood? No, it really is a bad idea."

"Child stay here," Vel said stubbornly.

"I wouldn't be able to leave my kid behind if I had one, and I sure as hell don't belong here myself," she insisted. "Besides, the amount of time it takes to have a baby far exceeds the time it takes to rebuild a broken boat. There's no way I'd want to stay here that long, and the crew isn't going to hang around and wait for me either."

"Seven or eight turnings of the sun?" he scoffed. "They not wait for that? And then, you always have my smell. Always be welcome by tribe."

"You think it takes only a week to make a baby?" Jean asked incredulously. "Does the sun work differently around here or something, or maybe you're tracking the moon instead? That must be it. That would be seven to eight months if you meant that. At least it's much closer to reality."

"I know difference between sun and moon. Mean sun," he insisted. She was still in his arms, but now his hands had moved down to cup her buttocks instead, pressing her body upwards so their two sexes were flush against each other. Since he was so much taller, this action lifted her feet up so that her toes were barely touching the floor.

"Oh!" she gasped as he carried her back to the furs, kissing her all the way. "No, no, wait! I don't—there's no way I'm letting you—please, I don't—"

She was on the furs underneath of him, protesting with her mouth as her body drank in every single move and responded in kind. She was about ready to rip off the leather pants he was wearing, remove her jeans, and have at it, but her mind was screaming at her to stop.

"You have sex before?" he asked her then.

"N-no!" she gasped, blushing hotter than ever. Sad but true, she had never taken the time to explore that particular type of terrain. Which was a waste, really, since she knew most guys thought she was pretty hot. That's probably why the captain had been panting after her as well, more than likely.

The fact that Vel was asking her this question, however, did not bode well for her continued existence as a virgin. Not that she was particularly averse to finally ridding herself of a useless hymen, but it didn't follow that she also wanted to do the other half of what he had in mind. She was not ready for motherhood, either in one week or in one year. She wasn't even finished getting her doctorate, she still had two years.

"Vel, please, we should stop," she whispered as she felt one of his hands pulling at the buttons of her fly. Only the fact that the five little pieces of brass remained an enigma to him had kept him at bay so far. She could tell he was coming very close to ripping at them the same way he had ripped her shirt before. "I don't want to make a baby when I don't intend to stay. Children deserve to have both of their parents."

Sighing, Vel let go of her and moved away. He went over to another part of the room where a natural indentation in the rocks jutted out somewhat like a sink. When Jean followed, she saw that it was filled with water. He dipped in his hands and used them to get a drink, then smiled and moved over so she could do the same.

While Jean drank, he said. "We discuss later? Time to go eat."

"Yeah, I guess we could discuss it later, but I'm really not going to change my mind," she insisted as she followed him to the entrance. He moved aside the fur that covered it and held it open so Jean could step through, then wrapped a protective arm around her waist as they continued on into the great cave.

"Remember, talk only to females," he said. "Safe to talk to females."

"Will they even know what I'm saying?" Jean wanted to know.

"Mostly not," he shrugged. "I take you to my mother. She protect you. You ask her more."

"Finally, a good idea," Jean smirked. "She must have some idea how I would be able to leave here. Although, since she's still here too, and you're a fully grown man, that doesn't make that theory quite as sound as it seemed, does it?"

The two of them stepped through the entrance into the main cave. The eyes of about sixty people turned in their direction. The women continued to stare at Jean curiously, but every man there looked circumspectly away. It seemed as though she had already been claimed.

Chapter 3

Even though her shirt was ripped open and hanging loose so people could see her bra, none of these people noticed, unless it was just to cast a strange look at the fabric itself. Doubtless they all thought the gaping shirt must be perfectly natural for her kind, since they obviously were aware who she must be.

"Vel, did any of the others make it to these caves?" she asked him as they walked. "Nobody seems very surprised to see me here."

"They not reveal thoughts on faces," he told her. "Would be… rude?"

"I see," Jean nodded. "So if my gaping shirt was in any way offensive to them, they wouldn't let on to that, either?"

Smirking, Vel took the fur on his shoulders off in a very ostentatious manner and rather sensually wrapped her into it. The action made Jean's toes curl, to tell the truth. She wondered just how long she would be able to resist this guy if he kept doing things like that. Her hot blush was too telling, and the smolder in his eyes gained even more heat in response.

"We discuss later for sure," he said huskily in her ear before he let her go. He took her by the hand instead, leading her before Trip as if asking for his permission for her to be there. The two men conversed with grunts and signs for a bit.

"What did he say to you?" asked Jean as they moved to sit down at a nearby hearth.

"He say you may sit among honored hunters as my mate," he told her, smirking slightly as she blushed again "He say five others from ship here. One badly hurt. Lost arm to Jerris same time I find you. Other hunter bring him in. He almost with spirits, but hold to life."

"The captain's still alive?" Jean scoffed. "Unbelievable!"

"Jerris want to eat him," Vel continued. "Say he marked as his."

"Wait, you mean that—that tyrannosaur is in here somewhere?" Jean gasped.

"Jerris a hunter," Vel explained. "He not go against Trip's choice, but very angry."

Just then, a rather large, brutish sort of a Neanderthal swaggered over to where they were sitting and made a big show of smelling the air near Jean. She cast Vel a somewhat concerned look while the guy circled her a couple of times, looking her over.

"What does this guy want?" she asked uncomfortably.

"That Jerris," Vel told her, keeping his eyes on the fire. "He think he should get you, too."

The brute thumped his chest with one hand and extended the arm out to Jean. She cringed away from him, latching onto Vel's arm rather tightly and casting the intruder her most unwelcome stare.

"Not claimed?" he rumbled, glaring at Vel. "Why?"

Vel reached up and ran his fingers over the stitches on her head. "She hurt. Claim now, mate later."

"I eat!" Jerris bellowed hotly. "My right!"

"No. You not mark her," Vel growled back. "Mine."

Jerris threw back his shoulders and glared, but made no move to do anything more. "Take outside?"

"No. Already claim," Vel insisted. "Go away."

Trip stepped over and gestured at Jerris to sit down. Suddenly becoming meek and compliant, Jerris sat down across from them at the same hearth. All the while they were there after that, he frequently cast them a contemptuous glare.

"Must mate, or he take," Vel whispered in her ear, trying to explain the situation. "He claims right to all outsiders. Protects the tribe."

"So, it's either make a baby with a really hot guy, or what, be forcibly taken by some other guy who wants to have me for lunch instead?" Jean asked. "What happened to option three?"

"Jerris not let anyone leave," Vel sighed. "Not want more people led here."

"Not leave?" Jean gasped, her heart beginning to race.

"Hush," he said, glancing around. "Talk about later. You want ship back, we find way. But must keep you safe first. Must mate, or you die. Understand?"

"You have got to be kidding me," Jean said, shaking her head. Looking up to see a woman who was clearly a modern female in her fifties, Vel smiled and moved away from the two of them as she sat down. It was obvious the woman had heard what they were talking about, and had come to speak with her.

Smiling warmly at Jean, she said, "Hi, I'm Diana, Vel's mother. I'm sure you must have a great many questions about all of this. My son would like me to explain a few things, and I think you'd feel a whole lot better knowing them, too."

"Yeah, I'm sure I would. I'm Jean Moncrieff, an American student," she explained. "Okay, so what do you know about this place? I mean, from where I'm sitting it's pretty crazy."

"It's the lost world, I suppose," she shrugged. "A part of Pangaea that never kept up with the rest of the planet, or so I've been told. I really can't understand it myself, even after all this time, but these people have some sort of magic that governs it all. I heard you and the others are paleontologists. It seems a fair bet that if you survived you could sure learn a heck of a lot more about the past in a place like this."

"So, how did you get here, then?" asked Jean curiously.

"Once upon a time, among my many other pursuits, I aspired to be a movie star," she smirked. "Our ship was headed to Bermuda to film a movie, but we ended up here instead. The producer was ecstatic about the setting and we went out onto the beach to shoot a few scenes. Unfortunately, Jerris showed up and ate my co-stars, and then took me back here to store for a snack later. My mate bought me from him for the meat of ten kills, and here I am."

"But you had no say in any of it?" Jean gasped.

"As to that, while Jerris was keeping me for his snack, I'd made eye contact with Gruff, and I could tell that he liked what he saw," she said. "Admittedly, I flirted with the guy in hopes of avoiding my fate."

"But how did you even know what your fate was at that point?" Jean wanted to know.

"Both Jerris and Trip have been the guardians of this island for as long as anyone remembers," she explained. "Jerris knew very little English thanks to someone who had been here before, but Trip knew enough of it to explain my situation to me when I first arrived. Anyway, when Gruff asked for me it was in their language, so I had no idea what was going on until he suddenly wrapped an arm around my waist and hauled me away to his cave. Things became pretty apparent then!"

"No doubt," Jean smirked, thinking of her recent interactions with Vel. "And you got pregnant right away? Okay, but Vel said something odd to me. He made it sound like I'd give birth in just one week if I got pregnant with his child."

"That's no joke, my dear," Diana said. "I found that out the hard way. It happens only among the shifters—those seated around this hearth, who are members of the hunt, not the other hearths where the non-shifters are seated."

"So not everyone can shift?"

"Goodness, no," she laughed. "Most of them don't. There are twelve hunters currently in the tribe, and the other fifty people are a mix of mankind in various evolutionary stages. I really don't know how that works, like I said. But Trip and Jerris seem to be the key somehow. The ones who seem to possess the gift to keep it all in order. Jerris would probably rather not allow you to live, but if you were to have a child with Vel and make no move to leave this place, I'm sure he would leave you alone."

"But what if I don't want to stay here?" Jean protested. "I have a life, you know. I have dreams, goals, aspirations, siblings and a mother. I don't want to just disappear off the face of the planet and leave them wondering what happened, thinking I'm dead when I'm really still alive."

"I do understand that, my dear," she nodded. "I was the same way when I first arrived. Gruff cured me of all that nicely enough, though. And I can tell that you're already very attracted to Vel. You wouldn't even have to learn to accept him. Trust me when I tell you this, if you make any attempt to leave this place, Jerris will kill you. No one has ever left here once they've arrived."

"Ever?" Jean gasped, biting at her bottom lip in consternation.

"Never ever," Diana assured her. "It would be foolish to even try. So I suggest you start getting used to the way things are, and allow yourself to enjoy it. Vel is a fine-looking man, and you two already seem to be very attracted to one another. Live, Jean. Live every day of a very long life in happiness and the security of knowing you are among the elite as long as you remain with my son. Doesn't that make a lot more sense than dying for no reason other than your foolish pride?"

"I—I'll think about what you've said," she said softly. "Thank you for your concern."

Diana got up and left again, leaving Jean feeling more confused than ever. She glanced over at Vel, wondering how he could have possibly told his mother anything, but then she figured out most of her knowledge was probably just knowledge of how things worked around here, and knowledge of reading the look on the face of a stranger.

"You like mother," Vel smiled. "She like you. That good."

"How do you know?"

"Feel it," he shrugged. "Good energy."

"I see," Jean said, unaccountably irritated now. She was feeling somewhat disheartened by Diana's words. She hadn't spent over four years in college just so she could become a subjugated cave woman who was always afraid that somebody was going to eat her or the child that she'd practically been forced to have just to survive. The whole thing was starting to really piss her off. She said, "Okay, I'd really like to go back to the cave and rest some more now. My head is really aching."

"Do not feel so bad," Vel said, rubbing at her temple. "Anger make head hurt more. All will be good. You see."

Jean cast him a doubtful glare before she looked patently away from him.

"I take you back," he said, tugging gently at a lock of her hair. "We sleep more. Make sure you feel good when we mate. Want you to feel good."

"Wow, that's really weird," Jean smirked. "Most guys are more worried about how they feel instead. I guess you're too primitive to be so selfish, huh?"

"Very selfish," he said as they began to walk away, and slipped a possessive arm around her waist to emphasize this point. "Only I make you feel good. Understand?"

Jean chuckled. "Yeah, now that part sounds very familiar," she told him. "I understand."

*****

Now that the two of them were alone in Vel's cave again, Jean was unaccountably nervous. He had promised her that she could get some sleep, but he had been just as adamant that they'd be mating sometime after that. And with Jerris copping such an attitude concerning her, and the words she'd exchanged with Diana still resounding in her brain, the whole situation seemed to be spiraling towards one inevitable fate.

She was about to get laid.

It was funny how young women always seem to fantasize about where and when that would happen. She'd managed to keep herself so busy all this time that she'd avoided the high school prom scenario, the first starting at college scenario, and any other scenario all the way up till now. It wasn't that she'd actively tried not to get laid, and she'd had offers—more than she could possibly count—it was mostly that none of them seemed appealing.

This offer, however, apart from the fact that it was unavoidable, was probably the most exciting one she'd ever had. Vel was tall, handsome, and gentle, and yet somehow she knew he could also be powerful and cruel. He had an aura about him that screamed 'don't take shit from anyone', and she was thankful he'd seen her as a potential mate rather than a potential meal, all things considered.

Snuggling back into the furs with him, feeling his arms holding her, Jean's body refused to cooperate with her intentions to sleep. It seemed that every single nerve ending was attuned to the man who was currently wrapped around her. Especially the nerves near where the two met near her butt and his groin. Those ones were firing off like it was the Fourth of July. She wondered if he noticed her heartbeat rapidly pulsing, or the slight tremble of her body which she couldn't seem to get under control.

"Jean want to mate now?" he asked softly in her ear, telling her clearly enough that he was well aware.

Blushing furiously, she tried to turn her face to where he couldn't see, but he sat up slightly and turned her onto her back, pinning her underneath him instead. Their eyes met and held, and then suddenly he was kissing her, his tongue easily prying her lips open so it could slip inside.

This time, Jean didn't feel any desire to protest. All of her desire had become centered on that area just a bit lower. Her pussy was throbbing with need, and all she could seem to do was cling to Vel's arms and return his kiss, which of course only made him kiss her even more.

A soft little moan caught somewhere in her throat when Vel pressed his rock hard cock against her thigh. A little frisson of fear reared its head just for a moment before her rampant need squashed it like a bug, leaving her completely at its mercy.

"Vel, I—" she tried to say, but his lips and tongue swallowed up whatever the words were going to be before she could even get them out, and her addled brain had no idea what they were going to be, so she didn't try again.

Vel's fingertips slid across her stitches briefly, then meandered down along her neck and chest until they found the hollow between her breasts. He fiddled with the fabric of her bra, looking for a way to remove it, and she quickly sat up slightly and unhooked it from the back so he wouldn't end up ripping that garment as well.

He tugged the bra free of Jean's body the instant it was lose, and then his hungry mouth found a new place to play. Jean sucked in a sigh of pleasure as his tongue came down to flick one of her nipples to life and then the other. She threaded her fingers through his hair, greedily holding his head in place. If she'd known it felt this good just to have a man's mouth on her nipple, she would have found a guy to do it for her much sooner than this!

Jean's hands slid down Vel's bulging biceps, gripping frantically as she sought to bring his lips to hers again. Reading her correctly, he did exactly that. The heat of this second bout of kisses far surpassed those of the first, and that was saying a lot. She couldn't help it when her nails bit into his flesh along the sides of his back—she just couldn't seem to get close enough, and she gripped a bit too hard in the attempt.

Vel tried again to work at the buttons along her fly, and Jean chuckled. She pushed him back enough so he could watch what she was doing, and demonstrated how they fit into holes by undoing one of them. Fascinated, Vel slid his pinky through the hole and tugged, and another button came free below the first. The puzzle now solved, he wasted no time pulling the other three buttons free.

"Those are called buttons," she told him.

"Buttons," he smirked. "Keep man out."

"Well yeah, I suppose so," she chuckled. "But also keep clothes on."

"Mostly keep man out," he replied, puffing up his cheeks again.

Jean giggled then, because now that the evil buttons had been conquered, Vel removed her pants with a rather smug expression. When he found her thong underneath as well, he tugged it down right along with them. She wasn't even sure he realized they were two separate garments as he did so until they came apart once they left her feet behind. He gave them only a brief glance before tossing them aside.

Jean stopped giggling. The carnal look he gave her then made her heart skip a beat, and then his lips crushed down on hers again. There was no mistaking the shift in the mood from playful to passionate. Every place he touched her—and that was everyplace—burned with the heat of her desire. She moaned softly into his mouth as his fingers came down to push inside of her.

"Very wet," he said slyly. Jean knew he was gloating at his abilities, but since he was doing such a good job she didn't feel the need to complain about it. Besides which, before she even had time to say anything he had removed the fingers, and now he was pushing his cock into her instead.

He was rather large, so the task was a bit painful and didn't happen all at once as she would have liked. But when he finally got it in, she felt only a moment of sheer relief before the pleasure kicked in instead. She whimpered against his shoulder as he started to move, but very soon she was moaning instead, mindless in her need. She wasn't sure, but she thought she'd actually bit his shoulder briefly at one point.

Again and again he thrust into her, and Jean was lost in it all. The taste, the touch, the belonging—all of it melted into her like it was the part of her life that she'd been missing all this time. In that brief moment, she would have loved to stay like this forever, just forget everything and everyone in favor of Vel. But then she came, hard, and came spiraling back down to reality with a crash.

She knew that she couldn't stay like this forever, no matter what her future held. She knew that she couldn't hold this moment in time and forget everything. Not when she was in a very dangerous world full of so many unknowns. Not when she was with a man who wasn't even fully human, but some sort of magically induced dinosaur.

Sure, she'd always kind of liked dinosaurs, but that didn't mean she wanted to become one's mate. Especially not in a place where women were considered nothing more than property, or maybe even nothing more than food. An outsider like her didn't belong in a place like this. Diana may have chosen a life here, but that didn't mean that she was going to do the same.

"Hey," said Vel softly, running a finger all down her nose and lips. "Not think so much."

"Who says I'm thinking?" Jean wanted to know.

"Your face," he smirked. "You thinking a lot."

"I've got a lot to think about, haven't I?"

"Think later, Jean," he told her. "Better thing to do right now. Think about this instead."

Jean hadn't expected Vel would want to do what they had been doing again so soon. But obviously, he was nowhere near done touching and tasting her, if his current actions were any indicator.

"Vel!" she gasped softly when he entered her again. If anything, he was even harder than he had been before. She muttered softly into his ear as he moved against her, not even sure what she was saying to him as she did so. Something along the lines of, "Yes, that's it. That's good, just like that. Yes! Yes!"

Vel was not quiet either as they moved together, but seemed to be answering her words, sometimes in English, but often in his own language. The soft, guttural tones were both soothing and intoxicating as they met Jean's ears. They touched her in a way nothing ever had before, bringing a prick of tears to the sides of her eyes.

"Want you, Jean," she thought she heard him say. "Wait so long for you. Knew you come here someday. Make you want to stay."

Chapter 4

Jean woke before Vel, and just like the last time, she made use of the facilities—if that's what they were called—while he continued to sleep. With nothing better to do, she decided to wander around the cave and look at the things he had in it. Maybe they'd give her a bit of insight on how a shape shifting hunter of the tribe lived his life prior to taking a mate.

Sitting on an outcropping that was flat enough to serve as a shelf, Jean spied what looked like three rocks that had been shaped into the likenesses of women. *Ah, he has a harem,* she chuckled to herself, though she was certain he'd be annoyed by such a thought. These little figurines were apparently very sacred to people in ancient times, so she knew better than to tease him out loud.

She did wonder, though, how it was possible that these people would still believe in such idols when they had already advanced to sewing together leather clothing. Not to mention, why had a cynodontian lizard, a creature which should have lived much earlier than humans ever did, also been present on the island?

There was much more going on here than a simple lost world. Surely if that was all it was, these people would have developed a culture of their own over time, not acquired skills from more modern homo sapiens as they seemed to have done. She had to wonder just how many boats had ended up here over the centuries, and what had happened to the people who were inside of them.

Some of them must have survived and taught the people here about their culture. That was the only explanation that made any sense.

Vel was completely naked as he stepped up behind Jean and nuzzled at her neck. He turned her to face him, holding her at arm's length as he stared pointedly at her abdomen. "Baby not take," he sighed as he moved to cup her chin. "Jean must want baby too."

"I'm sorry, Vel, I just don't know if I'm ready to have a baby," Jean said. "The idea of being a mother in just one week—I need to tell you, that's pretty scary. And how is it even possible?"

"Magic," he shrugged. "All shifters have magic from gods. That how we shift."

"Yeah, I get that, but it still doesn't explain how," she replied. "It sounds impossible. But then again, before I saw you transform into a velociraptor right before my eyes, I would never have believed that was possible either. And Jerris? How can he possibly be the size of a human in one form and become something as big as a tyrannosaur in the other? Where does he store all the left over matter he's not using in human form anyway?"

"That is secret I do not know," Vel admitted. "Very ancient magic. Jerris very ancient."

"Are you trying to tell me that he's been around since ancient times?" Jean scoffed. "Maybe even since this island was formed? There are just so many impossible things going on around here, how can you expect me to want to bring a child into this world when I'm not even sure how safe he or she would be here?"

"Be safe," he nodded. "Child will be among hunters. No one hurts hunters. Even Jerris not eat a hunter unless wounded beyond repair. Besides, in vision I saw daughter with you."

"Vision?" asked Jean suspiciously, remembering his earlier words about knowing she would come there someday. "What vision?"

"Future vision, saw you with me," he said, confirming her thoughts. "Saw children, much happy. Visions never wrong, Jean. You be with me long time."

"What?" she scoffed. "I don't want to be here any longer than necessary. I must get back to civilization. My mother will be so worried when she doesn't hear from me. If only my damned cell phone would work, that at least would be something."

"What is cell phone?"

"A device used to communicate with other people at a distance," she huffed, turning away from him and dipping her hands into the water, bring them to her face to drink. She used the rest of the water to wash over her face, cooling her heated cheeks.

"Little box that make noise?" he asked. "Trip took. Wanted to see how work."

"You let Trip take my cell phone?" Jean chuckled. "I sure hope it didn't ring, then. I can only imagine that conversation."

"Trip not talk to box," Vel scoffed now. "Not stupid."

"No, I suppose not," Jean agreed. "But I doubt he'll figure out how to give it power in any case. It'll probably die well before he has a clue how to use it. Besides, I couldn't pick up any sort of signal. Something must be blocking the satellite."

"What is satellite?"

"Big box floating far up in the sky," she smiled. "Carries the messages from the far away person into the little box. Really complicated stuff. I don't quite know how to explain it."

"You have much knowledge, like mother," Vel smiled appreciatively. "Maybe you help her to teach?"

"Me? Teach these people?" Jean said with surprise. "Well, I mean, I intended to become a professor, of course, but at a college, not a cave. And I thought you said they mostly can't understand me. And who would I be teaching?"

"Hunters and their women," he said.

"No, you said I cannot speak to men," Jean reminded him. "How would that work?"

"If Trip say teach, you may speak to teach," Vel said. "They understand that not showing interest. But only speak to teach. You do not want man's interest. He try to hurt me to get you. Understand?"

"But I thought you just said nobody would attack a hunter," Jean pointed out with a frown.

"Not attack, challenge," he explained. "Battle or barter only ways to take a hunter's woman. No way I barter you away. Want to keep."

Jean blushed at his words. Vel's hand came up possessively as he pressed her body back to his. He traced a line from her stitches and down her throat, then lower along the side of her breasts. When she gasped, he closed in, bringing his hands up to cup her breasts as he ran his lips over the prickly stitches instead.

Heat spread rather quickly through Jean's body as he moved to bend her forward above the water basin. Gripping her thighs, he drew her legs open just enough to allow him entry and then slid his hard, thick cock right up inside of her.

"Vel!" she gasped as she clung to the lip of stone that kept the water from flowing into the cave itself. His hands remained on her thighs, gripping her tighter as she began to squirm against him, wanting to feel him deeper inside of her even though she was certain he was about to split her in half.

Vel practically roared out a groan against the back of her neck. She felt him run his teeth and tongue down the skin, and it made her so hot she couldn't stop herself from coming. That didn't stop Vel from continuing to move in her, working her up into a mind-numbing bundle of nerves, thrashing backwards with every thrust.

"You take baby now," he panted, making her tense. He smoothed a soothing hand along her back. "Take baby now, Jean!"

When he came this time, deep inside of her, Jean knew somehow that she had complied. The feeling of the new life inside her was almost electric. Their connection was instant, and it was a love unlike any she had ever felt before. Somehow, by extension, it even encompassed Vel. She was fascinated and thrilled and confused and happy and angry all at the same time.

Vel gathered Jean into his arms and carried her back to the furs. They spent hours there, either sleeping or making love. More than once, Vel smiled and rubbed a hand over Jean's belly, and by the end of the day she was sure it had started to grow.

"Do I look bigger, Vel?" she wanted to know.

"Not for a couple days," he smirked. "Give time."

"So I don't show that fast?" she asked curiously.

"Show soon enough," he said. "Cover up. We go eat. Tomorrow, I go hunt. You stay with mother. Be safe."

Jean nodded and found her clothes again, while Vel donned his clothes as well. She wasn't at all sure she looked forward to another trip to the hearth, but that seemed to be where they had to go to eat. She was grateful at least that they cooked the meat before it was served.

*****

When meat and vegetables were set before Jean, she surprised herself by eating everything she was given ravenously, and then eating the food that Vel fed her from his plate as well. He was rather indulgent as he did this, and she caught him more than once smirking over at Jerris as if he was rubbing it in. She supposed all men probably had the tendency to be proud when their woman was pretty, but he was really laying it on thick.

"Are you trying to make Jerris jealous, Vel?" she finally asked him after his own plate was also empty.

"Of course," he smirked. "He want my woman. Can't take. This pleases me."

"You're terrible," she grumbled, and he leaned down to nip at the mark he had left on the back of her neck earlier, inciting the other man to growl irritably and get to his feet. He stormed off across the hall, making sure everyone was well aware of his outrage along the way.

"Know this," he agreed with a shrug. "Time to return to own hearth. Need rest up for hunt."

Nodding, Jean allowed Vel to help her to her feet. She figured she didn't need help as yet, but she might as well get used to it. She spotted Amanda Picket watching her across the way, and cast her a small smile. The woman did not return it, and she quickly turned away. Jean wondered at her reaction.

"That girl marked for food," said Vel grimly. "Jerris mark three girls. All kept by Anissa until Jerris decide."

"But that's terrible!" Jean exclaimed. "How can people be marked as food? We haven't been eating people, have we?"

"Only eat if hunt go bad," Vel said. "Probably not eat, probably give as mates or keep."

"So, does Jerris mate the girls he marks for food?"

"Yes, he has five mates. Three were food."

"And the others?" Jean wanted to know.

"Gifts," he said. They reached the entrance to their cave. The fur was already thrown back, and when they entered they found Trip inside. Both of them gave him slight, deferential bows.

Trip held up the cell phone to Jean, shrugging as if he was stumped.

Jean smiled as she took it in her hands and pressed the on switch. The battery indicator light was blinking madly. She tried to see if she could call, and the phone turned off completely. Sighing, she said, "It needs energy to work. Unfortunately, we don't have the power supply we were using on the ship, or I could recharge it and try again."

"Ship on shore now," said Trip with a nod. "We go?"

"Not rest before hunt?" asked Vel uncertainly.

"Not take long," Trip shrugged.

"Old one, your movements take long."

"Go, get what needed," he said then. "I wait."

"And Jerris?" asked Vel uncertainly.

"I give task in other direction," he smirked. "Must go fast."

"So he's letting us go to the ship?" Jean clarified.

"We go now, go fast," Vel nodded. "Not let Jerris see. He see, might try to eat."

"Why would he do that?"

"Ship bad," said Vel. "He protect island from ship."

"Let's go, then," Jean said. "And maybe I could even find some of my clothes."

Hand in hand, the two of them headed for the exit of the main cave. Once he was outside, Vel transformed into a velociraptor again, and bent down as if offering Jean a ride. Of all the things she ever thought she might be doing in her life, riding on the back of a dinosaur was not one of them. She held on tight as Vel made for the ship at the bottom of the cliffs, taking the same path the rest of the crew had used to climb up before.

A thought occurred to Jean as they went. She wondered if any others of the twenty member crew might still be alive somewhere. There were a few other caves along the ridge besides the one they had come from. She decided that she would ask Vel about the possibility as soon as they could communicate again.

A voice in her head replied, *you can communicate with me now, silly woman.*

Wait, what? How are you doing that?

Magic.

And what is your answer?

I will ask Trip when we return. He knows many more things than I.

How come you communicate in better English in my head than you do out loud?

You always have a question for everything, don't you?

Probably.

It's part of the magic, woman. Now hush, we are here.

When Vel had sprinted right up to the ship, Jean sprang off his back and through the large hole in the hull. It led right inside the Captain's cabin, where the battery was.

"Take this thing, and this as well," she said. "We'll put everything into a pack, and carry it all back. Let me go gather a few more things that might be useful."

"Hurry, Jean," he said. "Jerris not be gone forever."

"I understand," she said with a nod. Moving as quickly as possible, Jean grabbed her satchel of clothes and the novel that she hadn't finished reading, and threw them along with the fully charged battery with three outlets and tied them all inside.

"I'll hold this, you work on getting us back home," she said when she was done.

"No problem," he agreed, already transforming before he was even done. Jean jumped onto his back again, and they raced back up to the caves, making it back without any altercation. Jerris must not have noticed what they were doing, thank goodness!

Trip was still waiting in their cave. He had dozed off on the furs, and now Vel used his big toe to gently prod the older man's shoulder. He woke with a start and peered intently at the two of them before he sat up again.

"Went well," Vel told him, and Trip nodded.

Jean was already connecting the cell phone cord into one of the sockets, and thankfully it began to charge. Looking over at the inquisitive faces of her two companions, she said, "It's going to take a bit of time before there's enough charge to use the phone. And even then, with all the interference around here, I have no idea if it's going to work at all."

"Rest now?" asked Vel tiredly.

"Rest for hunt now," Trip nodded. "We meet again after."

"Yes," Vel agreed, again giving a slight bow of deference. Trip bowed back, and then he left, dropping the furs behind him. Jean understood by now that whenever the furs were down, the dweller of the cave was at home and did not wish to be disturbed.

"You make work, call mother?" Vel asked.

"Yeah, if it works, I'll call her," she nodded.

"Tell her okay, want stay with me?"

Jean paused, looking at him uncertainly. "What would my life be like if I stayed here? I know nothing of this place, nothing of your people or your culture. It's all such a mystery."

"You want study, why not study mystery?"

"Why don't we just get some rest, eh?" she asked then. She really wasn't ready for the conversation Vel was trying to have.

*****

Jean opened her eyes and stared at the ceiling of the cave. In the dim light of the fire's remaining embers, everything was bathed in red. Hazy, somewhat like her feelings about this whole situation. Stay here? In a strange, pre-historic world where danger lurked around every corner and she had to be careful to avoid talking to people based solely on their gender? Could she stand a life like that?

Her eyes wandered over to Vel. If there was any reason she might want to stay, it would have to be the man himself. Tall, handsome and surprisingly smart for a dinosaur. And then another hitch. This tall, hot, surprisingly smart guy wasn't even human. He was some kind of magical enigma. For all that he was funny, and he sure knew what he was doing in the furs, she wasn't even sure if once the full moon arrived he wouldn't transform into some weird creature and gnaw on her.

Of course, that was a complete exaggeration, but still. She couldn't believe that she had agreed to have a baby with some guy she didn't even know. A baby that she'd be birthing in just two weeks. She didn't feel pregnant so far, but if she only had two weeks instead of forty, she was sure to be feeling it soon enough. She had to be growing this baby by the hour instead of the day, didn't she?

Vel stirred and woke beside her, smiling when he caught her staring. "No time to mate now," he teased. "Time go to mother."

Jean nodded and sat up, checking to see if a day had made her show, but so far she didn't look any bigger. She glared at Vel when he started to chuckle and reached over to give her belly a rub as well.

"Next day or so you see," he said.

"A whole day more?" she grumbled, pouting playfully.

"Not make want mate, woman," he growled, leaning in to give her a kiss. It was a rather hungry kiss. It made Jean want to mate as well. But then Vel set her away from him and got up to drink some water before holding out his hand to Jean, indicating the entrance.

Sighing, Jean got up, pulled on some fresh clothes, and followed. The outer cave was abuzz with activity, mostly involving the males who tended to be at the hearth where they'd been eating. Jean saw that Jerris was among them, and when he saw her he scowled and turned away.

"He not bother here," Vel told her in a reassuring tone. "Not allowed here. Outside cave, fair game. Here, not touch."

"Another one of your weird rules, huh?" Jean said with a nod.

They reached the entrance to another cave and Vel made a grunting noise before he moved the furs aside. Diana was sitting on a chair in her cave, and a man, probably her mate, Gruff, was washing up at an actual clay basin nearby. Jean smiled at him in greeting before she remembered she wasn't supposed to.

Gruff puffed his cheeks slightly with amusement. "Not worry, Diana do same thing. Not easy to learn new manners after knowing others, yes? When alone we talk, I know you not want me to mate. Okay?"

"Thank you," said Jean, blushing as she glanced over at Vel. He was smirking at her.

"Father, we go?" he asked then.

"We go," he agreed. "Feed the people, maybe see if we find rest of crew?"

"How does he know about finding the rest of the crew?" Jean asked uncertainly.

"Just told him in mind," Vel explained. "Like talk to you before. But not make promise. Might not be safe to try."

"Oh, I see," Jean nodded. She couldn't decide if that was cool, or really creepy. Who knew what these telepathic types were saying to each other behind her back?

The two men exited the room, each of them stepping over to kiss their women good-bye. Then Diana and Jean looked at each other uncertainly.

"Well, what should we do today?" Jean asked her with a smirk. "Scrub leather? Make tallow? Invent the wheel?"

"Funny," Diana laughed. "I think I'm going to like you. It'll be nice to have someone around who knows what macaroni and cheese tastes like."

"Hey, I brought a box of that back from the ship," Jean chuckled. "And a little pot to make it in, too."

"You're kidding!" she gasped elatedly. "I am so there!"

"Too bad we probably have to use water instead of milk," Jean shrugged.

"I think I can handle that after all this time," Diana told her. "Let's get cooking!"

"Back to my place, then," Jean said with a smile, and Diana escorted her there.

About half an hour later, smiling at each other as they settled together on the furs near the hearth, each with a pottery bowl of food, the two women grinned like they were eating gold. In a place like this, where milk was non-existent unless you wanted to harvest it from a human, and where the main food on the menu was true dinosaur—or maybe even a human visitor—it probably was.

Chapter 5

All of the twelve hunters, each of them still in human form, stood at the exit to the cave. They were casting each other looks with varying degrees of emotional content. To an outsider, it would be obvious that there was a lot going on among the group—some were friends, some were enemies, some played active roles in the drama surrounding this fact, while others simply stood back to enjoy the show.

But not one spoke a word as they stepped out and transformed. Among them, Jerris and two others became tyrannosaurs, Vel and Gruff and several others became velociraptors, and some of the others took on other predatory forms. The velociraptors grouped together and headed for the forest. The tyrannosaurs headed for more open ground, where it would be a bit easier to roam.

With their special purpose still in mind, Vel and Gruff needed to find a chance to split off and veer back towards the caves, which they managed to do about halfway through the day. When they realized there were people inside, they turned human again before they entered. They found three other survivors holed up in one of the caves too scared to go out again and very hungry as a result.

"We bring you to secret caves, Trip take care," Vel offered.

"What's a Trip?" the male asked, confused.

"Are you a Cro-Magnons or are you Neanderthals?" asked one of the females curiously.

"You paleontologist?" asked Gruff, winking at his son. "You sound like son's mate."

"Your son is mated to a—a paleontologist?" she asked, shocked. "How did that happen?"

"Very recent," Vel shrugged. "You come now, we keep you safe. Not so safe later."

"Must warn," Gruff reminded him.

Nodding, Vel shifted into a velociraptor briefly before turning human again.

"What the hell are you?" the male asked aggressively, grabbing up the biggest available rock and chucking it right at

Vel's head. Gruff easily put out a hand to deflect it before it came anywhere near.

"Good job, Brad," scoffed the other woman.

"Hunters," Vel explained. "Others think you are food, but we make friends. You help fix phone for Jean. She want to call her mother."

"Are you going to help us get off this crazy rock, then?" asked the male.

"Too dangerous to try," Vel insisted. "Must not, or Jerris eat."

"What's a Jerris?" asked Brad.

"Big dinosaur, ate other friends," he explained. "No more talk, or he come back. Go now."

"You heard him, ladies, let's go," Brad decided. "Unless you'd rather stay?"

"We'll go," they both said together, and they all headed for the exit. Both father and son shifted, with Vel carrying the women while Gruff carried Brad back home as swiftly as they could.

They brought them straight to the shaman's cave, which had a secret extra cave behind it.

"Stay and wait," said Vel. "Not safe to go around. Wait for Trip."

"We will stay," Brad assured them.

*****

Jerris didn't return until a while after the new people had been hidden. Trip had gone to them to talk, but he did not share what had transpired among them with either Vel or Gruff. Both men knew that they would not return to that cave, and it was unlikely that they would personally see the hidden occupants within it again unless they were discovered or Trip decided to bring them out.

Vel decided it would be best not to tell Jean anything about finding them at this time. He did not want her to get emotional while she was with child or it could be harmful to her or their baby. With such a short time of pregnancy, it was even more important for her to eat well and avoid stress. Plus, he didn't want her to know they'd been attempting to build some sort of ship to leave. That, she didn't need to know at all.

He hadn't expected to find the women in his own cave when he stepped into it, but seeing the washed pot sitting on the shelf by his three ladies, he didn't have to work hard at figuring out why they were there. The pair of them had doze off on the furs, and Vel couldn't help but smile as he watched them sleeping.

Curious when he saw the strangely colored substance on his mother's bowl, Vel bent and swiped at it with his finger, tasting it. Pretty good, whatever it was. He licked the bowl clean and then did the same with Jean's, then set the two bowls next to the strange looking bowl they'd already put there earlier. He flicked it with his finger, and it made a sound, almost like a protest, making him jump. He composed himself quickly, hoping Jean hadn't seen the unmanly reaction.

When he glanced over again, he saw that she had opened her eyes. "It's metal," she told him. "Very hard rock."

"This rock?" he said, flicking it some more as he lifted it up. "Not heavy."

"I know, right?" she agreed. "Weird, but true."

Diana opened her eye and saw what they were doing. "Oh, Gruff's probably wondering where I am, no doubt," she said with a sleepy yawn. "I'll leave you two lovebirds alone."

"Good idea," Vel said, casting Jean a look that clearly told her what he had in mind.

"Don't forget, she'll be expected to help clean the meat in a few hours," Diana reminded him. "Bring her to me, I'll show her how it's done."

Vel nodded as his mother got up and headed out the door, grinning slyly as she let the furs fall behind her.

"She is really loving that you've got me around," Jean commented with a chuckle.

"Miss others like her," he shrugged. "Natural to do."

"Yeah, that's true," she had to agree. "So, just exactly how much meat are we going to have to prepare later, anyway?"

"That really what you want to talk about?" he smirked, sliding his hand over the stitches on her face.

"Those probably need to come out soon," she said, reminded by his action that they were there. "But that probably isn't what you want to talk about either, is it?"

"Not," he agreed, drawing her into his arms. When he kissed her, it was just a sweet brushing of the lips, making Jean sigh. Was he trying to make her want him? Maybe he hoped if he was sweet to her like this she might stop hoping to leave. But how could she want to throw away all of her hopes and dreams? It was just so confusing.

However, there was nothing confusing about the way she was feeling right now. As his hand slid down her body and around to grab her ass, she willingly moved against his hardening cock with a playful smile. "So, what did you want to talk about then?" she asked.

"Not need to talk at all if you not want to," he said, puffing his cheeks at her.

Jean giggled as he pressed her backwards until her feet hit the furs. She settled down onto them and he followed her there, pinning her to them. Their kisses grew hot and heavy as he moved against her, making her moan softly into his mouth.

"I like this talking," he told her with a smirk. His lips blazed a trail down the side of her throat, and he started pulling gently at the buttons on her shirt, remembering from before how they worked and figuring out how to push them through the holes.

"Me too," she admitted. She yanked on the leather cord that held closed the leather flap that covered the piece of anatomy she most wanted at the moment. His cock was hard and ready, and her mouth watered as she looked at it. Flipping around so that he was underneath her, Jean's mouth sought out that flesh, savoring it as she slid it into her mouth.

Vel moaned, shocked enough by the sensation to lose control. He writhed beneath her as she reared back and took him into her mouth again, all the way to his balls this time. Moving in a steady rhythm, Jean made sure that he wouldn't soon forget the pleasure she gave him.

Soon, though, he moved away and flipped her onto her back again. Jean grunted at the action, and then grunted again as he entered her. "Yes! Oh, that's—that's so good!" she gasped, and found herself clawing his buttocks in her attempts to get closer to him. Their bodies slapped together with a wet sound, and their moans filled the air. It was certain that their voices could be heard outside their little cave.

When she came, Jean laid there catching her breath for the few moments it took Vel to finish as well, and then he collapsed on top of her with a groan of delight. Then he smirked as he said in her ear, "Really good talk. Glad we had it."

Jean laughed, and Vel laughed with her. They spent the next hour snuggling until it was time to go.

*****

Jean had not been particularly excited by the prospect of preparing the meat, but the reality of it was much more disgusting. A pile of twenty small dinosaurs awaited the attentions of the women, and in the background she could also see several larger animals as well.

The sea of bodies were somewhat overwhelming, and Jean had to suppress a bout of nausea. They spotted Diana among the other six women, and Jean stepped forward to join her.

"I didn't even like going to the meat section at the grocery store," she admitted as she held a hand to her mouth. "All this meat I've been eating, before Vel got me pregnant I would never have wanted it at all, but it's almost like I'm craving it since last night's meal."

"It's the baby," Diana laughed. "You'll calm down a bit once you're yourself again."

"Say, I've been meaning to ask you," Jean said then. "What's it going to be like being pregnant for only one week? Have you got any advice you might want to give?"

"Well, I don't know what to say," she shrugged. "You know how they say every pregnancy is different? Well, when it comes to a pregnancy with one of the hunters, that whole thing just goes way beyond that. But I can't really begin to explain because I don't know which symptoms you're going to have, and I don't want to steer you in the wrong direction."

"I suppose that's fair," Jean said. "Well, what do we do with this meat, then? Just point me in the right direction."

"First we'll need to get the blood out," she explained. "Usually, the process goes bleed, skin, divide, cure, and store.

We'll be collecting all the blood to use for a really heavy soup base, then put all the vegetables the gardeners brought inside into it over the hearth inside of this huge pottery crock. We'll be keeping it boiling the whole time as we cure. Since you're so new to this, I'll have you help cut up the meat and stretch the chunks on sticks so we can set them near the fire so they can become slightly dehydrated over the next few hours."

"Sure, no problem," Jean agreed.

It took a few minutes before Diana gave Jean any of the meat. She showed her how to use the sharpened tyrannosaur tooth as a knife, explaining that she should try to save as much of the leather as possible so it could be prepared as clothing later. Then, they gave the skins to some of the other women to remove the fat off the back and prep to use, while Jean herself cut the meat into smaller pieces and skewered them. Then she set them all just outside the hearth fire so they could slowly cook.

While they were cooking, and the next dinosaur was still bleeding out, Jean busied herself with helping the other women cut up vegetables to throw into the pot. Then, when the next dinosaur was ready, she began the entire process all over again. It was exhausting work, but in the end the stew turned out to be delicious, and knowing that there was plenty of meat meant she didn't need to worry about the safety of her fellow shipmates in the near future.

Many hours later, or so it seemed to her, Jean was finally able to rejoin Vel for a small meal before they headed back for their cave. Sensing her exhaustion after her busy endeavors, he slipped a supportive arm around her waist as they went.

"So tired," she told him as she went straight to the furs. Vel smiled indulgently as she laid down and curled up onto her side. He joined her there, pulling her into his arms to hold her as they drifted off into slumber.

*****

The next time Jean woke, she glanced down at her belly and decided it was much more rounded than she remembered. Vel caught her looking down, and smiled as he ran a hand over the gentle swell. Jean smiled over at him.

"See, told you show today," he smirked.

"Yes, you did," she agreed. "So, what happens on the days you don't have to go out and hunt, anyway? Is there anything to do around here?"

"Make clothes? Make bowls? Clean out cave?" he suggested.

"I see," she nodded. "Well, I suppose it was too much to hope that you had a library around. At least I've still got the other half of that book to read."

"There is always sex," he added with a sly smile. "Plenty of time for that."

"My life is not going to consist of only eating, sleeping, sex, and giving birth," she said sternly. "I simply could not stand it."

"Understand," Vel said. "But no book here would interest you. Just primers to learn with."

"Do you ever read them?" Jean wanted to know. "Your English could still use some polishing up. Would you like to practice a bit more?"

"If you want to teach, teach others how to speak too," he said. "I go along, maybe learn as well."

"I wish to teach the women as well as the men, if I'm going to bother at all."

"Teach one, then other," Vel said with a shrug. "Plenty time in day for both. I speak to Trip, he arrange for you."

"That would be wonderful," said Jean with a smile.

"Want Jean to be happy here," said Vel. "Maybe want to stay."

Jean sighed. The trouble was, his plan seemed to be working. She hadn't given the least bit of thought to looking for a way off the island in over a day, truth be told. But did it follow that the lack of motivation to leave immediately meant she was thinking of remaining here? Not really. But with this pregnancy, she knew she couldn't hope to work on a plan of escape in the near future, and once she held the baby in her arms, who knew how she was going to feel about things then.

So maybe she should start looking for reasons that she should stay. It couldn't hurt anything just to consider the idea.

Especially since at this point there was no obvious means to escape anyway. And even if they repaired the ship, there was still no guarantee that they could use it to get off the island. If what Vel had told her was true, there was Jerris to contend with, and besides, who knew if there wasn't some sort of anomaly that would prevent the ship from returning to open water during the attempt.

No, there were a lot of factors leading to the conclusion that she might very well be stuck here, not the least of which of Vel's mother herself. If she had never managed to leave here, and she'd been here a great many years and never saw anyone leave this place in all that time, what chance did Jean actually have? And, with such a handsome man whose child she was having as the consolation prize, she figured things weren't all that bad even if she couldn't get away.

Vel kissed her cheek as he got out of the furs, relieved himself, and washed his face and hands at the little shelf. "I go speak to Trip," he said.

"All right, then," she smiled. "I'll clean up in here a bit and then read my book. I'd love to see what happens in the story next, anyway."

"You have story book?" he asked curiously, and she held it up for him to see. "No pictures here. Make much harder to read."

Laughing, Jean replied, "When you read that kind, the pictures you see are only inside your mind."

"I did not know such books were made," he told her. "Maybe later, I give this book a try?"

"I'm not sure you could follow it all," she said. "In the story it talks about cars, taxis, a skyscraper—all kinds of things I would have to explain to you, really. But if you're curious enough to sit through all of that then I imagine you could read the thing eventually. We can talk about it later, after you return."

Nodding in agreement, Vel headed out the door, closing the flap behind him. This was probably the first time Jean had been left alone since the first day she had arrived. Maybe that meant Vel already believed he could trust her to stay. And maybe that was because he was right.

*****

The way Jean figured it, Vel was probably going to snag her book to read later, so she hurried to finish it while he was gone. When she finished, she realized she had done nothing to clean up in their cave, so she quickly washed a few pottery bowls, shook out the furs so they weren't as dusty, and cleaned the potty chair up while she was at it. When she finished that, she even cleaned herself and some of her clothes, which she laid out to dry near the hearth fire.

All of that took a while, and she was beginning to wonder why Vel had not returned. Of course, she knew it would be foolhardy to go look for him, so she stayed put, but still she couldn't help but worry over his continued absence.

In reality, Trip had brought Vel and Gruff along with him to speak with Brad in the hidden caves. The man was insisting he wanted to build his raft and at least try to get off the island.

"It very dangerous to try this," Vel explained, casting Trip an uncertain glance. "Jerris will make you his food if you get caught."

"And who is Jerris, anyway?" Brad wanted to know.

"Hunter Jerris become very big," he said. "Jean call him ty— tyran?"

"Tyrannosaur?" supplied Tabitha.

"Yes, that," Vel nodded.

"You're saying if we try to leave, a tyrannosaur will try to eat us?" gasped Nicole from Brad's other side. "I hate this place!"

"Calm down, woman," Brad told her. "He's saying if we get caught trying. That's not to say we would get caught, right?"

"Very likely," said Trip then. "Jerris know many things. He see whole island inside head. Be glad he don't see you in here."

"You're telling me that a psychic tyrannosaurus is going to notice us trying to escape and eat us so we can't get away?" Brad asked.

"Yes, that right," Gruff nodded.

"Okay, my ability to believe all of this is tempered by the fact you two became dinosaurs while trying to bring us here, but how the hell can somebody transform into a T-Rex?" Tabitha demanded.

"Any shifter could learn to do," Vel said defensively. "Trip has done."

"This guy can shift into a T-Rex?" Tabitha scoffed.

"He horned one only when shaman," Gruff said. "T-Rex when hunter. He not hunt anymore. He keep time now."

"What does that mean, keep time?" Brad wanted to know.

"Connect time forward, connect time backwards, remember all of time," Gruff said. "Like father before him. All the people depend on him to keep history."

"Sounds like a really big job," said Brad.

"Very big job," Trip agreed. "Can even use magic to make you dinosaurs, too. But this is rarely done."

"You shift because of magic?" asked Brad. "And you could use that magic on others so they could shift, too? That is so weird. It's very hard to believe."

"Can show," Trip smirked, and he reached out to touch Brad. Light flowed from Trip's hand and into his body. "You can shift now."

"No way!" he gasped.

"Only work when you believe," he said. "You practice, gift come to you."

"Th-thanks, I think," Brad said nervously. "I never expected anything like this to happen to me, though. I'm not sure how to feel."

"Stay calm," said Vel. "We visit you sometimes, show you how to use. Right, father?"

"Yes, we can do this," he agreed.

"But how am I supposed to return to society as a shape shifter?" Brad pointed out. "And won't I end up needing to eat more meat or something?"

"More meat, yes," Gruff agreed. "Return, don't try. Not worth giving your life to try."

"Wait, are you saying we're stuck here forever?" Tabitha gasped. "I don't want to stay here forever!"

"Let Jerris eat you," said Gruff with a shrug.

"What!" she gasped.

"Not want to stay, can't leave, let Jerris eat," he repeated. "No more problem."

"How rude!" she snapped.

"Don't worry about it, Tab, we won't be staying," Brad said. "I promised you girls I would get you home, and I'm a man of my word. We need to build a raft. Once it's done, then we can figure out how best to use it. Right, Trip?"

"Humans are foolish," said the old man with a shrug. "But I will help you all I can. Even try to distract Jerris when you decide to go. I will send wood gatherers on a special run, they will bring here. Long as Jerris doesn't know, all will be well."

Chapter 6

Jean's stomach was growling and she was starting to get bored by the time Vel came back into their cave. She didn't think it would do any good to ask him what had taken so long, so she opted to refrain. Maybe if she didn't pry, he would offer the information of his own accord.

"Trip say you teach men next rising of sun," he said. "Almost time for big meal. You ready to go eat?"

"Um, yeah," she said. "Say, you said something about making bowls. I don't suppose you could bring me the things I'd need to make those next time you're gone for hours on end?"

Well, she hadn't exactly pried, right? She hadn't exactly complained either. Did cavemen pick up on subtlety?

"Sorry," he said. "Trip had other business he involve me in. Nothing that interest you."

"Are you sure?" Jean smirked. "I have a pretty inquiring kind of mind, and you guys don't strike me as the type of people who would put out a newspaper."

Looking at her almost guiltily, Vel decided yet again that it was too risky to let Jean know about the three shipmates they were hiding. Especially since Trip had granted their request for wood to build a raft. Vel wondered if the fact Trip had given the male the shifter gift would help to shield them from Jerris and his wrath, but he tended to doubt it. So the last thing he would want was for the mother of his child to be involved in any attempt to leave. As if he'd ever wanted her involved in anything to do with leaving before then, either, he reminded himself.

"What are you thinking about so hard, Vel?" Jean asked him. "You look like you've got the weight of the world on your shoulders. Whatever business Trip's got you involved in seems pretty important, to have you so worked up."

"It's—nothing," he insisted. "We go eat."

Vel held out his hand invitingly, and Jean took it, allowing him to bring her with him out to the fires. At some point his hand had released hers, so that by the time they reached the hearth of the hunters his arm was completely around her waist. A placement which was not lost on the rapidly angering Jerris as they approached.

Jerris was looking pointedly at Jean's belly until he realized she'd caught him, then he quickly looked away. He wasn't meant to be staring at another man's possession at all according to the rules and customs of this place. Jean wondered if he was really upset that he couldn't eat her, or if his real issue was that he couldn't have her for a mate. But really, it didn't matter much either way.

The two shifters must have been exchanging words mind to mind, since they were looking at each other so intently and their expressions were changing in a manner similar to a conversation. A heated one, by the look of them. Nervously, Jean moved away from Vel and moved to sit with Diana and Gruff as the two men continued to glare.

"Want challenge!" Jerris shouted angrily, drawing the attention of the others in the crowded cavern. "Want challenge now!"

"Not have to comply," Vel said, placing his hands on his hips. "Already claimed. Not owe you fight."

Baring his teeth angrily, Jerris stalked forward to press his nose to Vel's. Vel didn't back up even one inch, but moved forward instead, adding his own force to the contact. Their eyes glared at each other from less than an inch apart as each man seethed angrily.

"Stop this!" Jean shouted then. "Jerris, I don't belong to you. Leave Vel alone!"

The entire cavern fell silent as the stunned people just stared. They had heard that this Jean who was now mated to Vel was like Diana, but Diana had never done anything so bold in all her time here. The two men turned to stare at Jean as well, Jerris shocked and Vel annoyed. She knew she had disobeyed him, but Jean was so upset right then that she didn't even care.

Trip stepped over and used sign language and grunts to speak. Basically he said, "This woman, I allow to speak," he explained. "She will teach the people about modern life. All of the people. High time we stop living in past, move into future instead."

"No!" Jerris shouted as he too began to sign. His grunts and signs meant, "It is the past which has always sustained us. It is in the past where the source of all our magic lies. The future is uncertain and full of dangers. This island, our home, it is a simple place, and we have simple ways. If you let this happen, who knows what might befall the people? And we are so very few compared to what we once were. You should not let her."

"Jerris, I know that we two have been entrusted with protecting and teaching the people," Trip insisted. "Since my job is to teach them, they will learn what I choose, not you. These people will not be injured in any way simply by learning to communicate better. It's past time that the women became just as capable as the men. Seeing this girl, and others like her, it's easy to realize women are much stronger than the ancestors supposed. She shall teach everyone to become more like her. The strength of the people fails because only half of them participate in its maintenance. The spirits have shown me a new way, led by this girl, and I will not deny them their will."

Vel, who had become just as enthralled by these words as the others, had failed to tell Jean what was going on. She still stood there, seething fiercely, her eyes snapping with fire, and he forgot to watch the conversation as his gaze took her in. Could there be anything more beautiful than a woman exhibiting her strength and determination? If so, Vel had yet to see it.

"We come here to eat," Vel pointed out then. "We eat now. Talk another time."

"Yes," Trip agreed. "Vel is right. There's no need for all this hostility inside the caves. Jerris, if you continue in this manner, I will set you outside until you mend your ways."

Jerris turned and sat down abruptly, an action which Jean could understand. However, she had no idea what anybody had been saying up until then.

"What the heck is going on?" she complained.

"We eat now," Vel said, drawing her down to sit with him on their side of the fire, as far away from Jerris as possible. He didn't even look in their direction again for the rest of the evening.

*****

"What was all that about during dinner?" Jean asked yet again as she and Vel entered their cave later that evening.

"Trip told Jerris you teach the tribe so he must leave alone," Vel explained. "He say you teach all the tribe so we can move into modern times. Tribe got by with old ways long time, but numbers not so much anymore. Want women to become valuable, like you. Women much stronger than we thought. You humans show Trip that—my mother, then you. But mostly you. Beautiful, smart, not afraid. Want all women like this."

"Wow," Jean laughed. "That sounds like a really tall order. You know, Vel, not all the women would have the ability to be like me. Some would be afraid, not strong, maybe need the help of a man more."

"Know this," he shrugged.

"I need to take out these stitches," said Jean as she ran a finger over the side of her face.

"Me help," he offered.

Jean nodded, and took the little suture kit out of her bag of things. This time she got the clippers out and showed them to Vel. "The point on the bottom goes between the stitch and the skin, preferably without poking the skin. Moving it like this, once it's there make a cut on the stitch so it can be pulled out of the skin. Understand."

Vel nodded and made quick work of the task.

"You're really good at that," she told him. "You'd probably make a good nurse."

"Good," he smirked. "Now nurse this."

His hand slid down her body and rested between her thighs. Jean's eyes lit up with interest, since she'd been feeling somewhat horny all day anyway. She was pretty sure her hormones were on overdrive thanks to the accelerated pregnancy.

When Vel kissed her, she willingly surged forward into his arms. Kissing her all the way there, Vel guided Jean back onto their furs, then laid beside her as his hand moved over her baby bump, grinning wryly.

"How is this going to work, anyway?" Jean wanted to know.

"More than one way to fill a woman," he said, demonstrating by turning her onto her side and thrusting against her.

Jean groaned at the contact. "I think we are way overdressed, Vel, don't you?"

"Yes," he agreed. The pair of them wasted no time at all in getting rid of their clothing and regrouping on the furs again. They kissed passionately, hands exploring wherever they could, until Vel finally moved Jean so she was facing away from him.

Her heart was pounding hard just knowing what he would do, but Vel didn't do it right away. Instead, he ran his lips along the side of her neck, then nipped lightly on the spot he'd made before, suckling slightly. Jean suspected he was making sure it remained noticeable, and she giggled in response.

Vel grabbed her hips and held on as he pushed his eager cock into her from behind. Jean yelped with pleasure and arched against him, making it go in even deeper. They moved together with an intensity that left both of them trembling, faster and harder and better with each thrust. The feel of it was so incredibly good that there was no way either one of them could possibly stifle their responsive moans.

"Glad you come here, Jean," Vel whispered into her ear as he moved. "Very, very glad you here. Want you here always."

Jean's heart lurched at the words. She realized with a start of surprise that it was because she agreed with him. She actually wanted to stay. The orgasm that followed only served to reinforce the thought as she curled up against Vel, safe and warm within his arms.

*****

The next day, with Diana's help, Jean set up a sort of classroom where she could begin to teach the people as Trip desired. Her first class consisted of eight men, and one of them was Jerris himself. She couldn't help but feel nervous having him there, but he seemed to behave himself in the same manner as the others while he was there.

"How many of you guys actually know any English words?" Jean asked the group, and Diana did not interpret the question. Half of them nodded their heads, and the other half looked at Jean like she'd bumped hers. It was easy enough to know which was which from these reactions.

With Diana interpreting this time, Jean continued, "Sometimes the best way to learn a language is to start out with objects, so right now I'm going to teach you what I call each of these things. Once I do, I want each of you to practice using the word for the object whenever you use it from now on so you won't forget, okay?"

Diana handed each object to Jean in turn as she named a bowl, a cutter, leather, sinew, fruit, meat, and rocks. Each of the men were asked one at a time to repeat these words. Then, as she dismissed them, she reminded them that they could ask each other for help to remember, and they departed, replaced by eight more people Jean also taught the same lesson. This continued all through the day. Surprisingly, the women knew many more words than she had expected them to.

"How is it that you women talk so well?" she wanted to know.

"Diana been teaching for years during work," explained Anissa, puffing her cheeks with glee. "She tell us modern women have say. Wish that true for us too."

"Well, believe me, ladies, if I have anything to do with it, you're going to start getting much better treatment around here than you've had to date," Jean scoffed. "But for now, are there any words that you would like to learn that you haven't asked about before?"

"Don't you think it would be better to learn what they call some of the things around here instead?" Diana suggested. "Maybe it would be wise for you to learn to understand how these people communicate as well, so you are not left so completely out of the loop."

"Yes, of course," Jean agreed. "I hadn't thought of that, since they don't use actual language for descriptions. How do you describe something if it isn't even in the room?"

"We have words, if you pay attention," Anissa shrugged. She picked up a bowl and made a guttural sound, but as she repeated it several times Jean came to realize she was in fact using a very primitive sounding word rather than a simple grunt. She showed her several more objects and gave their names as well.

"Now you try," Diana encouraged with a smile. Jean did her best, and got quite a few sounds right the first time. "Wow, you're a natural. It took me much longer to get their language down."

"That's probably why you taught them your own," Jean said with a smirk.

"Now, it's time to prepare the dinner," Diana announced. "Would you like to help?"

"Only if there's no human on the menu," Jean replied, making the other woman grimace.

"Fortunately, that doesn't seem to be the case," she replied.

They spent about an hour roasting meat and using sharp rocks to chop roots similar to carrots. Then they brought all the food out to the different hearths, and they each went over to the hearths they were meant to sit at. Diana and Jean sat together waiting for Gruff and Vel to arrive, enjoying a companionable silence.

After the trouble they'd had the night before with Jerris, tonight's meal seemed remarkably quiet by comparison. Jean remembered that earlier when she'd been teaching his group,

Jerris had dutifully recited the words along with the other men, though she was certain it was only because Trip had told him to.

She didn't think that the uneasy truce they'd seemed to form during the lessons would last, and yet when he arrived before Vel he didn't even look at them. Jean was somewhat surprised until Diana explained.

"It would be very rude to look at another man's mate while he was not even there to see it," she said. "For all that Jerris is cruel and forceful, his belief in following the rules is of paramount importance to him. Tradition is everything. That is why he dislikes us so very much."

"I understand," Jean nodded.

The two men joined them soon afterwards, and they ate a leisurely meal together. Afterwards, they didn't leave immediately, but stayed to watch as Trip told the tale of Diana's ship when it had come so many years ago. Jean realized that she was almost able to follow it, especially with Diana clarifying the words as he went along.

"We return to cave now," Vel finally said in Jean's ear. She had a pretty good idea what Vel wanted to do once they returned to their cave. It was difficult to miss the particular sparkle in his eyes as they got up to leave. It became even more apparent what he had in mind when, before they even made it to their entrance, he snuck up behind her and wrapped her into his arms.

"What are you doing?" she asked with a giggle.

Vel smiled as he said, "What do you think?"

"Didn't you tell me there was some sort of rule that said we can't show emotions in public?" she reminded him.

"Yes, but already showing anyway."

Jean's jaw dropped when she heard this, and her cheeks were stained with a deep red blush. "I can't believe you said that," she gasped.

Vel puffed his cheeks at her, making her laugh. Then he ran little kisses down the side of her neck as the pushed the fur aside and stepped into their cave. It wasn't empty.

"What are you doing in here?" Jean demanded as she stared at Captain Luke Claiborne lying on their furs near the hearth.

"I've come to discuss our departure from this island," he explained, taking in the size of her belly as he spoke. "However, by the look of things, I doubt you're in any condition to go. How the hell did I miss that before?"

"Because it wasn't there before," Jean said. "Amazing as it sounds, this pregnancy started just three days ago. But why don't you tell me what you came here to say anyway. I'd like to hear what you have in mind. Maybe Vel can offer some advice."

"Then you've decided to stay?" asked Claiborne shrewdly.

"I—" Jean began, realizing how close she'd come to saying that she had. "I'm considering it," she amended before she blurted out her words in haste, and the tension in Vel's shoulders went from hopeful to slumped. Jean's belly filled with butterflies and she felt a strong desire to go to the man and confess that she did not want to leave.

"Why would you be doing that?"

"Well, the child for one thing," she explained. "I don't think he or she would do well if I brought him with, and I don't really want to leave him behind either. And, the only real reason I would want to go home aside from my career would be my mother and my siblings. If I was sure they weren't worried about me having gone missing at sea, I believe I would have no qualms at all about staying here."

"What if I promised you that I'll get out of here?" Claiborne asked. "That I'll contact your mother somehow and tell her where you are and how you are doing? What then?"

"How would I know you'd succeeded?" Jean sighed.

"I'd come back here and tell you, of course," he said with a nod. "I sail these seas every day, remember? If I can find my way off the island, I can find my way back again."

"Even with only one arm now?" Jean asked doubtfully.

"I promise you, Jean, I'll get off this rock, call your mother, and come back to tell the tale," he said solemnly.

"Maybe got better idea. Maybe we make phone work," Vel pointed out. "If phone work, you talk to your mother that way. Not need to risk this man."

"You've got a cell phone here?" asked Claiborne. "That would sure be helpful if we could use that instead."

"Yeah, at least until the phone bill comes due," Jean sighed. "Maybe I could get my mother to keep paying it, what do you think?"

"Can she afford to?" Claiborne asked.

"I suppose so," Jean said. "And I'm sure she'd be willing to keep a line open to her youngest daughter, right?"

"If we can get a signal," Claiborne added. "That's the toughest part. If we could, though, maybe I could just call in somebody to fly me out of here, and you could just tell your mother your whereabouts yourself."

"What about if we went to the top of the mountain?" Jean asked him.

"Now that's the clever girl I've come to admire," said the captain appreciatively.

"Jean belongs to me," Vel growled, baring his teeth slightly.

"Calm down, Vel," Jean told him. "The captain and I have already discussed that matter, and come to an end to it, have we not?"

"If you say so," he shrugged. "Having a woman is the least of my worries right now. I'm more worried about getting a proper dose of antibiotics and some proper surgery to fix this stump. Unlike you, I very much need to get off this island if I hope to survive. However, I'm more than willing to try to establish communications for you if it means maybe I could get a chopper to pick me up. But Jean, do you really think you can climb up there in your shape? You look like you're very nearly ready to have the baby, weird as that seems."

"Vel thinks I've got another couple of days before the baby is due, and I'm more than willing to try," she said. "The only real problem is how to climb up the mountain without Jerris breathing down our necks. He's sure to notice what we're doing way before we reach the top."

"Ask Trip to make Jerris protect us on journey," Vel said. "He can't eat us if Trip make him our protector."

"That's a brilliant idea!" Jean agreed.

"We go slow for Jean, and for captain," Vel decided. "Both need to move with care. Not want arm to bleed again, not want trouble for baby. Not want baby born on mountain."

"That's for sure," Jean agreed.

"Very well, then," the captain said with a nod as he got to his feet one-handed. "Vel, if you would be so kind as to escort me back to Trip. It was difficult enough just getting here like this. I'm not too sure I can make it back on my own."

"Jean get rest while wait," Vel said. "Want to talk to Trip, get all this planned. Will return when all ready. We go tomorrow, captain's arm not wait."

"All right," she agreed as she watched them go.

Chapter 7

"It hasn't worked so far because we couldn't get a signal from the satellite," Claiborne explained to Trip a little while later. "We need to go somewhere we're more likely to be able to pick it up."

"And if you go to highest place on island you get 'signal'?" Trip asked curiously.

"Yes, that's right, if we can manage to pick it up," said Claiborne with a nod. "At this point, I don't see any other way I'm going to survive. I really appreciate all that you have done for me, sir, but I simply must ask for this one last thing. If you do it, the cell phone will remain here when I leave, and perhaps you'll even be able to use it to contact the outside world yourself."

"Amazing device," he said with a nod. "But who would I want to call with it?"

"You could get someone to drop off some supplies," he suggested. "Foods you don't have to hunt down, or maybe clothes made out of fabrics such as ours. The possibilities are endless."

"You make good point," he nodded. "Time to become more modern if we want tribe to survive. We must learn modern things, why not have modern goods too? And you say you want Jerris for protection on way?"

"My idea," Vel nodded with a smirk. "Can't eat us if busy protecting us."

Smirking slightly as well, Trip said, "True. I like idea. Get you safely to top and back and I not have to distract him either. Too bad raft not done or it be good time for others to escape."

"Others? What others?" asked the captain.

"He won't survive if he tries to go with them instead," Vel pointed out.

"Go with who?" Claiborne wanted to know.

"Three of your shipmates Jerris not find," Trip said. "They make a raft, want to leave if I distract Jerris. Maybe this distract him, but raft not ready. Not sure done soon enough to go before Vel and Jean return. Have to think of another way."

"I see," Claiborne nodded. "But I simply cannot wait around here any longer to buy them time, sir. The infection has already set in. Even your best medicine isn't slowing it down."

"Know this," he agreed. "Must go at the start of day. I will speak to Jerris, he will do as I say. No worries. Now, get rest. Vel return with mate in start of day, yes?"

"Will be here," Vel nodded.

"Sure you should take her now?" asked Trip with concern. "Baby close."

"We return before birth," he insisted. "No worries."

Trip made a sign of acceptance, and Vel bowed as he left the two men alone and returned to his cave for the night. Jean was sleeping when he got there, so he simply curled up beside her and fell into a deep sleep.

Although it had been a while since he had seen the visions—not since the woman involved in them had arrived—as he slept that night, he dreamed of Jean and their daughter once again. She had green eyes, just like her mother, but her hair was as dark as his.

*****

When Jean awoke the next morning, she was substantially bigger, and hungrier than she could ever remember being in her lifetime. So hungry, in fact, that if a rat had scurried past her right that moment, she was pretty sure she would have chased it down and ate it right then and there. Definitely had to be the baby who wanted to eat that.

"I've got something for you, Jean," Vel grinned as he crawled out of their little nest to step across the room and grab a leather pouch. Inside was some cured meat. "Knew you would hunger greatly today, so have plenty meat and fruits to take with on journey. Want to eat something now?"

"Yes, I really think I do," she said, practically snatching a morsel of meat from his hands. Vel puffed his cheeks in amusement as she gobbled it down, then gave her another piece to go with the first.

"We go to Trip now," he said. "He tell Jerris about chore this morning. Jerris sure to be upset, but he always do what Trip says. No worry that he will say no."

Jean nodded, then went to use the facilities before stepping over to wash her hands and face. Vel dumped the bowl onto the fire, and it momentarily sputtered before it continued to burn. Then he added more fuel and banked it so it wouldn't burn out while they were gone. This had the side-effect of making the room much hotter, but they left so soon afterwards it hardly mattered.

Jerris and Trip were already arguing with each other when they arrived at the door, so the pair opted to stand outside and wait for the furor to die down. Eventually, Jerris stalked out the door and found them there, casting them both a disgusted but resigned stare. Captain Claiborne followed fast on his heels, already carrying a light pack which contained the food and medicine he would need for the short journey.

"I go speak to Trip before we leave," Vel told the two men. "Come, Jean."

They stepped inside, and Vel briefly signed with Trip before they went out again. He said, "We go now. Hope takes only day or so, get Jean back before baby comes."

"Don't think this mean we friends," Jerris grumbled. "Still eat you someday."

Jean glanced at him with a smirk as she replied, "Thanks."

Jerris curled his lip at her and said no more.

Vel led the way out into the main cave, past a group of curious onlookers, and onward towards the exit. They did not shift forms, but remained human-looking as they headed for the path they needed to begin their climb.

"Might get cold near top," said Jerris. "You bring furs?"

"We have furs," Vel answered, and the other man nodded. They had little else to say to each other for a while until they stopped to pick some berries along the side of the road.

"Eat here, rest a bit," Jerris said to Claiborne, not looking in Jean's direction. She didn't know if this was because he hated her, or because it was customary not to make eye contact with a female. Either way, in her currently huge and irritable state of being, she didn't like it. She didn't tell him that, though, since she wouldn't want to push her luck.

Jean sat on a boulder and stretched out her legs, which were aching terribly. So was her back, her belly, and even her arms. Plus her head was pounding. Her body was bulked up to the size of an eighth month pregnancy without the benefit of getting used to it gradually, and she was definitely feeling it now.

"We get further up mountain then break for night," Jerris said. "Should go now, get done for day before sun drops from sky."

"Slave driver," Jean grumbled.

"What slave?" he wanted to know, then remembered again he wasn't supposed to ask.

"A person made to do what another person wants even if they did not agree to do it," she supplied, though he had already turned away.

"Then, am I not slave in this?" he pointed out. "Not what I want to do."

"You have a point," she had to agree. "So let's just get this over with."

Vel offered his hand to help her to her feet again, and he put an arm around her waist to help her along the way.

They went on like that until the sky began to darken, and then they reached a smooth, flat cliff with plenty of room for all of them to lay down. Vel laid a fur down for him and Jean to lay on, and then brought out a few more furs to cover them up, which he set aside until they wanted to sleep.

Jerris made quick work of starting a fire, and then they each brought out something to eat. As they did so, Captain Claiborne suddenly broke out into song. The other men were fascinated by this, and sat watching him. Meanwhile, he had brought out the herbs Trip had given him to use and threw some into the bowl he'd brought along for that purpose. He put water in the bowl from the animal skin, then threw in the herbs, setting everything near the side of the fire to warm. Eventually he used a piece of thick leather to pull it out again.

"That funny words part of healing spell?" Vel wanted to know.

"No, my friend, but it certainly helps to heal the soul," Claiborne replied. "I'm hoping that the gods will find the music to their tastes and let me live through the night."

Jean placed a hand on Claiborne's forehead with a worried frown. "You're really burning up, you know that? I hope we'll be able to get you to the top at all, sir. I need you to get this damned phone to work, because I certainly don't have a clue."

"Funny how a scientist with a PhD doesn't even know how to work her own cell phone," he smirked, and Jean saw that his glazed-over eyes were traveling slowly down her body while the other two men were signing quietly to one another behind him. Jean saw Vel looking at her, and she quickly got up and went to him.

"I hope he's going to make it," she sighed. "Those medicines Trip gave him make him seem pretty out of it. I have no idea what condition he'll be in by morning."

"Must make sure he survives," said Vel. "If he die, you won't know how to fix phone, right?"

"Exactly," Jean said with a nod. "He told me he was going to boost the signal, and much as I know a great many things, the inner workings of a cell phone and all its functions is not a part of that knowledge base."

"I will use magic to make him last," Jerris said decisively. "But you promise that once you use phone to talk to mother, you not want to use it again? Not use it to call outsiders onto this island?"

"I promise you that I am only trying to call my mother," Jean replied, omitting the fact that Claiborne had other intentions for himself. "She must be worried sick about me by now. I normally talk to her every single day."

"I worry much for the state of this place if more outsiders come," he said. "It happen before, and tribe very nearly died. This even before Vel's mother come. Not want this to happen again."

"I understand," Jean nodded. "You really care about your people. Just like my mother really cares about me. Understand? She worries for me like you worry for them. I must set her mind at ease."

Without another word, Jerris turned and held a hand above Captain Claiborne, who was currently doing his best to continue sitting in an upright position but very close to losing the battle. His palm glowed with a golden light, and then it shot down into the captain so quickly that Jean wasn't even sure she had seen it happen at all. Claiborne fell backwards with a thud, and Jerris tossed a fur on top of him.

"He sleep until sun comes again," he said then. "Rest now. Long journey then, and must hurry for your sake. Babies come on their own time, not yours."

Jean nodded and laid back on the furs next to Vel, who was still sitting up. He said, "I take first watch, you rest."

"I am protector," Jerris protested. "No rest until task done."

Vel nodded, knowing better than to argue with him. Still, he was unwilling to sleep since he didn't know if Jerris would try to break the phone to protect the tribe. He hadn't promised to protect anything except the people, after all.

"Not worry," Jerris signed to him. "Will not stop your mate's call."

"Very well," Vel signed back, and he settled down beside Jean, trying to sleep as well.

*****

The following morning, the four of them woke with the sun and began their climb in earnest. It took a few more hours to reach the summit, where they set down their things and pulled the cell phone and its power generator out of the large pack Vel had been carrying. Vel set the entire assembly onto a flat portion of rock, and Claiborne sat down beside it, fiddling with a few switches and buttons.

Static finally cleared, and then they could hear a voice. It sounded like an irritated woman.

"Who is this?" she demanded. "Why do you keep calling here?"

"It's me, Mom," Jean said. "I've been trying to get a clear signal. I'm on an island somewhere near Bermuda. Our ship was caught in a storm."

"Jean? Thank goodness!" she gasped. "When do you think you'll be home, sweetheart?"

"That's the thing," she said. "I've met someone down here, and I've decided to stay. I don't have a lot of time to explain it, I just wanted to let you know that I'm okay."

"Wait, what do you mean stay?" she began, but the static returned in full force, and only a dial tone met their ears when it finally went away.

"Do you want me to get her back again?" Claiborne asked tiredly.

"No, I've told her what I came to say," Jean decided with a nod. "I think I need to start heading down again. I'm not sure how long I have until the baby decides to come."

"I'll never make it down again," said the captain, giving Jean a wink that Jerris did not see. "Perhaps I'll just stay here and enjoy the view. Go ahead, you three, and leave without me."

"Then we may as well let the phone die along with you," Vel said decisively. "There's no more use for it now."

Claiborne nodded and tossed the little box onto the ground, then eased himself down as well. Everyone but Jerris was aware of his plan to wait a bit and then try to call for someone to come get him. If he tried to do it while the dangerous shifter was present, it was likely he'd be eaten for his efforts. As Trip had told them all, do nothing that would be deemed a threat to the tribe or Jerris would eat first and ask questions later.

"I do not like to separate," Jerris signed at Vel.

"He's dying," Vel replied. "Why have him slowing us down?"

To Claiborne, Jerris said, "Seems like waste of food to leave you here, but Trip said not to kill. Maybe I come eat you sometime later."

"Thank you, Jerris," he said. "You're all heart."

"Don't tempt me," he replied. Then he grabbed up one of the packs and began to walk. "Come with now," he called over his shoulder.

"Make sure you wait until we're well out of earshot," Jean whispered. "Jerris is sure to hear otherwise. Good luck."

"You too," he replied.

Jean and Vel quickly grabbed packs and followed to where Jerris waited just beyond the rise. None of them spoke as they made their way carefully down. At one point, Vel transformed into a velociraptor and Jean tiredly climbed onto his back, bringing both of their packs along for the rid. Not long afterwards, the distinctive sound of a chopper ripped through the air, making all three of them look up.

Glaring angrily at Jean for a moment, Jerris suddenly shot upward into the sky, his shape rapidly going from smallish human to huge dinosaur in an instant. He turned and began to hurry back toward the top, but by the time he got halfway back there the chopper was already leaving. Jerris was so mad that he let out a furious bellow. Before he realized what was happening, the cliff face of the rocks there shattered, and the ancient dinosaur plummeted down to the watery depths far, far below.

Jean gasped when she saw this, and then Vel increased his speed, intent on returning home. They managed to enter the cave and go straight to Trip's cave, looking for the old man there.

"I see that the two of you are back, but where is your protector?" asked Trip as Vel returned to his human form. "Is anything amiss?"

"I am not certain," Vel signed. "Jerris fell off the mountain and into the sea."

Trip's eyes went wide at this, and he nodded gravely. "I do not think he would die, any more than I would," he signed back. "He is certain to return here to tell me what has transpired."

"The captain got away," Jean added even though she didn't know what they were talking about. "A chopper flew in and took him. Or, at least it flew in and I saw him dangling as they flew away. They were getting out of there because they saw Jerris, more than likely. He was running straight up the side of the mountain in full dinosaur form, ready to eat them if he'd been able."

"I do not doubt it," Trip smirked, then looked Jean over speculatively. "We should bring you straight to Diana. She help women have babies, and you look ready for help."

"Sort of feeling that way, too," Jean nodded. "So I take it the birthing process takes less time also?"

"Not really," Vel said apologetically. "Might take longer, body has less time to prepare."

"Great, now you tell me," Jean grumbled. "Come on, let's go. Old man, bring me a potion to ease this pain, will you?"

"Diana will make special women's potion for you," he said. "No worries, okay? You do fine."

"Thanks," she nodded, and followed as they headed for the entrance and up the way to where Diana and Gruff's cave was situated. When they stepped inside, Diana already knew exactly what they wanted. Jean was sure somebody must have told her along the way.

Chapter 8

After getting done with the process at last, Jean came to the conclusion that while there hadn't been any complications, giving birth seemed to take a very long time. Not to mention, parts of her body that she hadn't even realized she had seemed to be aching fiercely, and when Diana brought her the pain medicine she asked for she was more than ready to swallow the whole thing.

Her daughter had been lying next to her so she could suckle, but at the same time she took her medicine, Diana also brought the baby over to the warm water she'd prepared and cleaned her up. She could see her curly, dark hair and smiled, thinking that Vel would be pleased to have made at least that much of a contribution. She hadn't looked at her closely enough to determine if there were any others.

Vel, Gruff, and Trip were all standing just outside the cave waiting to be allowed inside. Of course, as the tribe's leader, Trip was meant to have a look at the child first. It was up to him to determine whether or not she would be allowed to remain among them, or if she should be set outside. Not that anybody expected him to throw the girl out, of course.

"Trip?" said Diana as she stepped over and pulled the fur aside. "My granddaughter is cleaned up and ready to meet the shaman now."

Vel smiled at this. He had not been told until just then that his child was a girl. Not that he'd expected any other outcome, since the visions were always correct, but it was still nice to have it confirmed. Now, he had to wait until Trip gave her a name before he could hold her in his arms.

Trip stepped ceremoniously into the cave and crossed the room to where the child lay waiting. With a smile of greeting he lifted up the squirming baby and looked her over, finding a birthmark that surprised him.

"Can this be?" he gasped, staring at it for a few moments. "Is it true?"

"What is it, Keeper?" asked Diana nervously as she watched him.

"Look here, Diana," he signed as he pointed out the mark. She also did a double-take and looked more closely. "Is it a talon shape?" he wanted to know.

"I believe so," she signed back excitedly. "Will you accept it?"

Trip nodded. "I wanted to make a change," he signed. "What better way to start that than to accept a girl to be a shaman for the tribe? The gods have chosen her, just as surely as they once chose me. We will gather the tribe and tell them what has transpired."

"As you wish," Diana agreed, and then she turned to the entrance again, but turned a second time to ask, "What will you name this child, then?"

"She is as her sign says," he signed, then raked one hand downward, in other words saying, "Her name is Talon."

"Talon," repeated Diana in English. Then she ushered in both Vel and Gruff, who were looking at her as if she had gone completely crazy.

"You said it was a girl," said Vel, confused.

"She is a girl," the old man said. "Talon."

"That's a boy's name," he pointed out.

"It is a shaman's name," he insisted, and showed Vel the back of her arm, where the small V shape dominated. "She bears the mark. I accept the will of the gods, and so must you."

"I accept her willingly," he agreed, and held out his arms to receive her from him. "But who knocked out my mate before we could even talk?"

"Leave her be," Diana said. "She needs rest after all that she'd been through. Especially since she went through it right after climbing a mountain, so I've been told. What were you thinking, bringing her up there?"

"It was mostly to rescue the armless man," Vel signed with a shrug. "He needed our help to get the medicine he needed, or he would have died. Nothing we have here would have kept him alive."

"He could have contacted Jean's mother himself, and let her know," Diana pointed out. "You didn't need to bring her there as well."

"It made her happy," Vel shrugged. "Have you not yet noticed that making her happy pleases me greatly?"

"Just because I don't possess the sight doesn't make me blind, son," she admonished him. "Of course I have figured out how happy the girl makes you. And how happy you make her as well. Now, have you slept at all since the two of you returned, or did you spend the whole birth pacing by my door?"

"Pacing," he admitted.

"Go on, lie down with your mate and baby and get some rest," she said. "I'm sure all of you can use it. Trip will probably decide to present her to the tribe in a while, and I'm sure you'll want to be awake for that."

With a proud nod, he agreed. Then he carried Talon over and set her beside Jean, curling against them both as he settled down for a well-deserved sleep.

*****

Amanda was sitting beside one of the hunters at the hearth fire when Jean and Vel brought baby Talon into the main cave later that day. At Trip's request, a small leather dress had been made for her to wear for the upcoming occasion. Since her mark was in full view on her arm, Talon's clothing would not need to be removed to reveal it.

Jean was a little nervous about it all, since she wasn't even used to being a mother yet, and already her child would become the center of attention. Their focus on Talon would bring more focus on her—not that she wasn't getting plenty enough already. Many of the people she'd been teaching the other day had brought her items they wanted the names for, so she'd been supplying words to them periodically almost every time she turned around.

Thankfully, some of the other members of the tribe had begun taking up the slack, giving words in her stead whenever they knew what they were. Anissa had begun to teach words to the women while they worked on making the meals or cleaning the caves, for which Jean was very grateful.

"Why are you over here?" Jean asked Amanda curiously as she took a seat next to her.

"Just before he left with you the other day, Jerris bartered me off to a hunter," she explained. "I'm not exactly sure what his name is, since I've only seen the sign for it, and nobody has even bothered to talk with me at all since I began to sit here. Most of them have been ignoring me completely."

"That's surprising," Jean scoffed. "I know that Diana would have welcomed you at the very least."

"She didn't come to eat on the night I was mated, and she was busy helping you last night as well," Amanda pointed out. "So tonight is the first time either one of you has been here. Also, I really wanted to say sorry for not talking to you the other day. I was told it wasn't allowed."

"Yeah, I wasn't sure about that," Jean said. "I thought you were mad or jealous or something."

"Oh, I'm sure I was jealous," she admitted. "Everything always happens so easily for you, and the rest of us just follow in your shadow, right? But I suppose I'll forgive you, since our kids will be growing up together and all."

"You let him make a baby in you?" Jean smirked, stealing a glance at the man she'd mated. He wasn't a cute as Vel, of course, but at least she didn't have to pity her as she would have done if Amanda had become a mate to Jerris.

"Oh, Amanda, have you been mated to Furr?" said Diana happily as she came to join them.

"Oh, is that what he meant when he was pulling on his beard?" Amanda chuckled. "That's good, then, because for half a minute I was worried his name was Lice or something!"

Jean's eyes went wide as she suppressed a laugh. "That good, huh?"

"I didn't say he had any," she grumbled, smirking again. "Actually, things seemed to go well other than not knowing how to communicate."

"That's good," said Jean. "I'll make sure to have Trip send Furr as one of my next students so we can teach him a few words, okay?"

"Will you see if he will allow me to help teach, too?" Amanda asked. "The more the merrier, right? Oh, Trip is motioning to Vel. What is going on?"

"He's about to announce Talon's gift," Jean smiled. "If you were jealous before, I'll hate to see what you're about to do now."

"Do I even want to know?"

Vel had already brought Talon to Trip at his beckoning, and the shaman was gesturing emphatically as he held out her little arm for the others to see. Most of them just stared in stunned silence. Then, just before Trip had finished his speech, Jerris stepped into the cave, staring at all the commotion with a confused frown.

"Jerris?" Trip signed. "Are you hurt?"

"I'll live," he signed as he took a seat. As Vel stepped over again, Jerris motioned to him to see the baby. "What name does she bear?"

"Talon," said Vel, earning him a stare.

"Is it a boy?" he asked.

"She is a shaman," said Vel.

Jerris stared at Trip as if he had bumped his head, and Trip stared right back at him, daring him to say anything about it. Instead, he turned his eyes back to the girl as Vel lifted her hand to show him the symbol on her arm.

"I see," he acknowledged, deciding to keep his thoughts to himself.

*****

Over the next few days Amanda and Jean started teaching Furr how to talk. They also realized that most of the other hunters tended to tease him about his name, which they learned he'd gotten because he was born with so much hair. Even now, he seemed to cut his beard much more often than they did in an attempt to keep it under control. Jean asked Vel to take Amanda and Furr to the ruins of the ship to grab a bunch more things, and the sewing kit with the scissors was among the newly obtained supplies.

Today, Talon was a week old and Amanda should have had her baby over a day ago. Instead, she and Furr were sitting among the women's class so Furr could keep learning as Amanda took the scissors to his beard and hair, giving him his very first real trim. They were both curious to see how the other men would react to him when she was done.

The gatherers returned with more wood, and as she'd noticed on two other occasions over the week, they had brought long lengths of wood with them towards Trip's cave, looking over their shoulders nervously as they did so.

"Okay, now I know something is up," Jean grumbled, stopping mid-lesson to just watch.

"Make raft," said Sheena, a gatherer among the group.

"Raft? What do you mean?" Jean asked curiously. "Why would anybody around here want a raft? Have you suddenly decided you want to go fishing or something? And where would you have ever heard of a raft anyway."

"Not tell you," she shrugged. "Trip hiding outsiders. They want raft to go."

"Really?" said Jean, moving to pick up Talon as she began to fuss. "How many people know about this?"

"Trip, some gatherers, Gruff, and Vel," Sheena said, though she signed each of the names in case her pronunciations were not good enough.

"Vel knew about this?" she asked, her stomach clenching with ire. Why would he have failed to tell her about finding some of her shipmates? She felt a keen disappointment to know he had not trusted in her decision to remain here. Maybe he still feared that she would try to leave if she knew about the raft. She wanted very much to seek him out and discover the truth.

She asked, "How long have these outsiders been hiding here?"

"Long time," she said. "Almost same time as you."

Now the pieces fit a little better anyway. She had asked Vel and Gruff to search for survivors during the first hunt, but they never said anything about it again when they returned. She'd thought they must not have found anyone, but obviously they had found them, and brought them here to hide. And supplied wood for them to build a raft.

"How can they use a raft to leave, anyway?" she scoffed. "Jerris is sure to eat anybody who tries to go."

"Heard Trip ask other two girls if they go," she added. "Jerris sure to stop food's escape."

"No, if I know Trip he intends to distract Jerris," Jean said with a shake of the head. "He'll send him as far from the raft and its occupants as possible. But I'm surprised he said nothing to Amanda or me."

"He already know neither want to go," she pointed out.

The two women cast each other a dubious glance. Sheena had a point there. Both of them had pretty much decided that motherhood and hot guys sounded a lot more fun than probably death just to go back to a society which demanded much more of a person than they'd ever have to tolerate here. Sure, women were subjugated here, but the two were also determined to change that while they were at it. So yes, Trip was quite right to assume neither of them wanted to go.

"Trip's a pretty smart dinosaur," Amanda smirked.

"Not dinosaur," Jean replied. "Only becomes dinosaur while teaching the tribe."

"Stop channeling Vel and tell me what we want to do about him keeping a secret," Amanda smirked. "I know you better than to think you're going to just ignore it."

"Oh, I don't know, Amanda," Jean sighed. "I think he was just trying to protect me, don't you? I'm sure anybody who goes on that raft is going to get eaten or drowned or something and never make it back to civilization. He wouldn't want me to go, that's for sure."

"Yeah, but he should have let the decision belong to you," she pointed out. "We can't let these men treat us like our thoughts and feelings come second. If they start out like that, they'd still be doing the same thing twenty years from now."

"I hate to break it to you, Amanda, but these men have already been treating women like that for a hell of a lot more than twenty years," Jean pointed out. "It's probably going to take us a lot more than twenty years to liberate the women around here."

"Yeah, but we owe it to our sisters to try," Amanda insisted.

Jean rolled her eyes at this. "Why do I get the feeling you would have been all over the women's lib movement if you'd been alive back then?" she grumbled. "Fine, I'm just going to tell Vel how disappointed I am that he didn't trust me. It won't be because I'm a woman, it'll be because I am a person and as such I deserve respect. I'm going to tell him that I understand why he wasn't ready to trust me yet, but in the future I'd like us to learn that trust in each other, because that's what makes a successful couple. Is that good enough, or do you think I should deny him sex and demand him to worship at my feet or something?"

"Damn, girl, calm down," she said with a cringe. "I like what you just said very much. It's probably the most awesome thing I've ever heard. And I want somebody to tell Furr I want to build trust between us, too. Hey, Diana?"

While Amanda was getting Diana's help with talking to Furr yet again, Jean asked them to watch Talon for a few minutes and excused herself from the others and went in search of her mate. She found Vel lying on their furs trying to read the book she'd left lying there earlier, and she couldn't help but chuckle.

Vel glanced up, surprised to see her standing there while she was supposed to be teaching. Their eyes met and held, and he realized somehow that she knew. As soon as the apology started to shine in his eyes, Jean stepped over and plopped down on the fur beside him.

"What is tower?" he wanted to know.

"People make places to live and work instead of using caves," she shrugged. "Why am I hearing about a raft from a different mouth than your own?"

"What would you want with a raft?" he asked, glancing down at the book again.

"Nothing," she said. "But I would have liked to know when you found my friends. I've been sad to think that they were probably dead. Besides, you left intending to look for them, so it's telling that you never mentioned that you found them."

Vel sighed and looked at her again. "Not want you in danger. Not want you to go."

"Vel?" Jean sighed, brushing a stray hair from his eye. "I know you couldn't trust me then, but I'd like you to trust me after this, okay? And I'd like to be just as sure that I can trust you. If you want me to be happy, that would be one of the best ways to make sure of it."

"I like that idea," he said, his lips quirking up into a smile.

Before she knew it, Vel surged up and pinned her underneath him. Jean giggled, grabbing her book and tossing it aside so she could lay down again.

"Where Talon?" he wanted to know.

"The women have her," she said.

"Good thing," he said, puffing his cheeks at her teasingly as the glitter in his eyes made a decided shift in its intensity and meaning. "Baby keep them occupied while we work on trust."

"I said trust, not thrust," Jean told him with a smirk.

"No different," he told her, bending to nibble on the side of her neck. Then he kissed her, and their tongues twined hotly together. Their breaths came in short little gasps as Vel rubbed against Jean's body in the most suggestive of ways. There was no way she was going to deny him when the heat between them built so rapidly, promising in its intensity.

Vel had gotten better at undoing buttons, and swiftly undid her jeans, which she'd only managed to fit again that very morning. It amazed her that her body had gotten back into shape so fast after the hyper-speed pregnancy and birth. She suspected that must be magic as well.

But that was the least of her concerns at the moment, when a very hot and very needy man was busily yanking her jeans right back off again. She moaned softly as she worked his pants downward as well. Vel didn't even wait for them to be fully unclothed. As soon as they both were uncovered enough to get the job done, he wasted no time before he pressed her down and entered her.

"Yes!" Jean hissed as he began to move in her, her slick juices aiding in the endeavor nicely. Again and again their bodies slapped together, the cadence in sharp counterpoint to the sounds of their voices as they mingled hotly together.

The feel of Vel's heart pounded against Jean's chest as he sat up and brought her with him. He grasped her hips and moved her up and down on him, and Jean latched onto his neck, holding on so she could help. They grunted with every thrust as they moved, and then Vel bit gently into the side of her neck, running his tongue over the spot, then biting it again, making her moan louder than ever.

"You like that," he smirked. "Remember from before."

Jean just laughed and nodded, threading her fingers through his hair. Then the two of them moved harder and faster than ever, mutually realizing they couldn't stay like this for the rest of the day. Vel pulsed into Jean's body as he came, and it set her orgasm off as well. When they were both calm again a couple minutes later they righted their clothes again.

"Better go back," he told her then. "I join you soon. But then have to go help friends move their raft, get ready to go."

Jean nodded, and headed back out the way she had come. She could seem to erase the smile on her face the entire way.

Chapter 9

Trip had come up with the perfect excuse to get rid of Jerris the following day. When Jean and Vel had come back down from the mountain, they had not brought the cell phone back with them. So Trip decided that he wanted to have the thing back, and he sent Jerris up after it As an added precaution, he also decided to have Brad and the others take the raft out to the water through an underground tunnel. He was certain that they'd be able to take it all the way through, since he had gone that way as a triceratops more than once before.

To help lead the way, he asked Gruff and Vel to come along with him, much to the annoyance of both their mates. Diana felt that Gruff had better things to do than go crawling through tunnels with the crafty old shaman, while Jean simply didn't want Vel to go because it was always possible that something could go wrong. Like the cave could collapse, or they could get lost, or who knew what else.

In the end, of course, both of the men chose to do as Trip requested. It was an honor to have been chosen by him to begin with, both had argued. And, added Vel in his most soothing manner, it was very unlikely that anything would go wrong.

"Remember you want to trust," he said to Jean. "Time to learn now, yes? I be fine, trust me."

Jean sighed. She couldn't possibly argue with him after he said that. Because this was the perfect opportunity to begin to practice what she had been preaching. Instead, she nodded and held him close for a few moments before she finally let him go. "Be safe," she said softly, and did her best not to begin to cry.

She didn't want to think about what was going to happen when Jerris returned and discovered that the two captives he'd had Anissa watching over were now missing. Everyone there had been instructed not to tell him what they knew, of course, but not all of the inhabitants of this place had a backbone solid enough to withstand the Neanderthal's roar. Surely he was liable to get one of the weaker members of the tribe to tell him something eventually.

Jean spent the greater part of the time that Vel was away sitting in their cave with baby Talon, rocking her gently and telling her stories about America and the life she'd chosen to leave behind. She even told her all about the study of ancient fossils and the curiosity she had about ancient land forms, made even more curious by the discovery of this very island.

Talon seemed to absorb everything she told her like a little sponge, her bright eyes alight with intrigue even at her young age. Seeing this, Jean no longer wondered if Trip was right about her eventual success as a shaman for the tribe. She was absolutely certain that the old man was right.

For his part, Trip was beginning to rethink his decision to take the raft through the caves as they cleared the third unexpected hurdle in their path. He had forgotten that while he was in his dinosaur form he was a great deal taller. That meant the ceiling was very tall and he'd easily cleared it, but he hadn't accounted for the fact that humans couldn't skirt tall objects that stood in their way, which for the triceratops would have been viewed as inconsequential.

"Maybe we should just have you turn into a triceratops and carry the thing," Gruff signed at the old man then.

Trip cast him a withering glance. He signed, "If I did that, I'd have to keep putting the thing down because I was barely clearing the roof of the cave. We just need to get past all of this part of the cave and enter the cavern. We'll get a long ways towards our destination once we reach that point of the journey. Just be patient, we're nearly there now."

"You made this sound a lot easier than it's turned out to be," Gruff insisted. "I am not well pleased by the difference between your words and this reality."

"Do you wish to turn back then?" Trip asked pointedly.

"No, that would take even longer to achieve," he signed back irritably. "Let's just get this done already. Some of us still have to go hunting tomorrow if you don't recall."

"The cavern lies just beyond that boulder," said Trip, indication yet another set of tall rocks to get around.

"I can't believe it!" Gruff signed, glaring at the shaman openly. "Come on, everyone, let's get around this one and then we can take a break."

"What did he say?" asked Brad tiredly.

"Go around that boulder, then take rest," Vel interpreted.

"Great," said Brad with a grumble. "Hey, I wanted to show you what I learned to do anyway. I wasn't even sure I'd be able to do it, but last night I grew a tail. I think I've worked out how to become the whole beast. I wondered if you'd watch me and give me a few tips on how to do it right."

"Sure thing," Vel agreed. "But why bother to learn if you're just going to go back to the humans anyway? You're not going to need to shift if you're there."

"Do you think your mate is the only person who needs some closure before she can just disappear?" he pointed out. "I might decide to come back here someday, you never know. The place has its charms."

"Like what?"

"Like being able to have two women do your bidding, no matter what it is, and they'll do it because they don't want to have to fend for themselves."

"Not very nice idea," Vel scoffed. "Woman better if she want to be there with you."

"Well, yeah, there is that, but I've been enjoying these two so much that I didn't give it much thought," Brad smirked. "I'm all about the ego, and everybody knows it. These two knew what they were bargaining for when they were the ones I saved."

There was no time for further conversation until the raft was successfully sitting on the floor of the huge cavern on the other side of the rocks. Then everyone sat down for a rest. Vel helped Brad learn to fully shift into a velociraptor, and then Brad also tried a stegosaurus on for size. They remained only a while longer while they ate some dried meat and drank from a water skin, and then they moved on again.

*****

Even in the form of a tyrannosaur, climbing to the top of the mountain took a bit of time. Currently, Jerris was about halfway there. Of course, he was less worried about the climb itself, and much more worried about why Trip had suddenly decided to send him. It had been quite a few days since the little box had been used to contact Jean's mother, and for the one-armed man to become the first person to escape the island in centuries.

Jerris was no fool. It was obvious that the old shaman had decided he wanted to make some big changes. He'd been trying to find ways to improve the tribe ever since he allowed Diana to remain and mate. He'd been watching Vel's progress over the years with a great deal of interest, and in many cases, amazement. He was much smarter than the non-shifting members of the tribe. Also, he thought of things that none of them would ever have come up with, and he didn't even realize what a powerful gift it was.

It wasn't a big surprise that the son of an outsider had mated outside the tribe, either. When compared to the appeal of the beautiful Jean, the women of the tribe failed in comparison. But he also knew that most of the women from outside didn't find him appealing, and he even had some idea why. He looked too much like an ancient man, while some of the younger members of the tribe looked more like the more modern humans. This was no accident, but a modification to the gods' design.

All the magic that the tribe accessed sprang from the same place. It was still a mystery why some of them had an ability to access it while others could not, but over the years it had often worked to Jerris' advantage. Not many others were able to learn how to use the site to rejuvenate and keep themselves alive, as both Jerris and Trip had done. The people they now watched over were all far younger than either one of them. Trip should have gone back to the spring a long time ago to renew himself, as Jerris did often, but for some reason he had decided to stop.

In fact, since the small body of water was on the way to his ultimate destination, Jerris decided to stop there now. He knew that if he drank this time, he was likely to transform his looks to those of the younger generation. He would look more like Gruff and Vel. He wondered fleetingly if Jean would notice him then, but he knew better and set the thought aside. It wasn't Jean he was doing this for—but perhaps one of the others might suffice.

He wasn't quite sure when he'd decided he wanted a modern mate. The though had entered his head here and there over the years, but seeing the mate Vel had managed to obtain put the thought back in again with a vengeance. If old Trip wanted to modernize the tribe, then he was going to modernize as well. Let the shaman say whatever he liked, there was no going back once the deed was done anyway.

Jerris transformed into his Neanderthal form and dropped down onto his haunches above the trickling water. He held out his hands to capture enough water to drink his fill, then brought it to his lips. He drank it greedily, and would have went after more except that as he began to move forward with that intent the first drink hit his system. His body froze, and he fell sideways onto the ground, writhing and kicking.

He knew from all the other times he'd been here that the transformation would take some time. Several hours went by before he was in control of his own muscles yet again, but when he sat up, he was no longer Neanderthal, now he was a Cro-Magnon man. He lifted up his hands as he stared down into the little pool, admiring himself. He pressed the ridge of his brow, reveling in the smaller size.

"Now I look good," he gloated. "Get modern woman for myself."

*****

Jerris stood at the top of the mountain in his new form, the cell phone in one hand and the charging box in the other. He was trying to figure out how Claiborne had managed to make the thing work, but he had no idea what had powered it, let alone how to work the thing once it came alive. Finally admitting he'd need help from one of the women, he sighed and set the thing down, turning into a tyrannosaur before he picked the two items up again.

Most tyrannosaurs found their forelimbs useless, but as an adapted hunter, Jerris had long since learned to make his arms useful for more than just ornaments. He palmed both the phone and the charger and began to head back down. His great, thundering steps loosened up some of the rock formations, causing an avalanche, but he ignored it completely as he continued on his way.

While all of this was happening, Trip and the others had just reached the mouth of the cave. Proceeding carefully out into the pounding surf, Brad and the four women he was taking along with him each carried a long pole which they'd be using to steer. It was the best they could do since it was not possible to make paddles with no tools.

Nicole and Tabitha had to urge both Stacy and Anne to move. The two women had been frightened of the wrath of Jerris for nearly three weeks now, and so they were deathly afraid to step out into the sunlight where they might be seen by their intimidating captor.

"Well, Trip, it looks like this is it," said Brad with a smile. "I'll get these girls out, like you want me to, and maybe sometime I'll return to learn more about this gift you bestowed on me."

"Yes, we will meet again," said Trip with a nod. "But by then, the state of this island should have changed. I have something to ask of you."

"What is it, old man?" he wanted to know.

"My tribe's numbers are smaller than ever," he said. "I fear the people may perish unless more people come to mate with them. If you return, I wish for you to bring others. Can you do this?"

"Sure, old man, I'll help you out," he said with a smirk. "Sounds like fun."

"This place here," said Gruff, pointing at the waves. "Water push against rocks. Have to get far down, end of land. Down there, water push you away from this place. That how Diana's captain planned to go. Planned, but Jerris stopped. Ate all who tried. Probably do same to you, but you try. Go outside rock there, then down to end. Only way."

"I understand," said Brad. "Come on, ladies, let's leave this rock behind."

All five people got on the raft and pushed off, heading for the gap between two large rocks as Gruff had suggested. Once they got through, they headed south, using their poles all along the way to keep from being swept by the wind into the rocks they wanted to clear. It was heavy, intensive work, and when they finally managed to reach the beach where their ship sat, they decided to come in for a rest and look for some supplies.

"Remember, we're in a lot of danger here," Brad said. "We have no idea when that Jerris creature might come down off of the mountain. Be quick, and be quiet."

Brad didn't have to tell any of them twice. He went directly for the food stores and grabbed whatever he could, stuffing things swiftly into a duffel bag. Each of the women also stuffed a bag, and they headed out again.

"We will tie all of these bags together and lash them to the raft itself," Brad decided. "We'll be much less likely to lose anything that way. There's no telling how long we'll be out on the open water. We should probably lash ourselves to the boat as well."

In the distance, they heard a thundering footfall echoing off the side of the mountain. Looking up, Brad could just make out the shape of a very large dinosaur nearing the bottom. They all gave each other a look of abject fear as the quickly tied the gear up and lashed it onto one of the logs, then brought along more rope instead of tying themselves on at that point.

"We're out of time," Brad said. "If we can see him, he's just as likely to see us. Move!"

As they pushed and shoved themselves back out into the water, the thundering footsteps began to grow louder and faster. They didn't take time to look, but it was almost certain that their little trip to the boat had come at a heavy price. A current grabbed their little craft and pulled it along. The poles were too short to do any more good, so the women each let theirs go as they'd already discussed before.

"He's coming!" Tabitha wailed. "I can see him on the beach!"

The giant dinosaur waded effortlessly out into the water and headed their way. Even this far out into the ocean, the water seemed to come up only to the beast's chest. All the women began to scream. Brad set the rope in Nicole's hands and suddenly jumped into the water. The raft nearly capsized as his body swiftly stretched to the same size as that of his foe.

"He's a monster!" Nicole screamed. "He's one of them!"

When Nicole dropped the rope, Tabitha caught it. She tried to stop the other woman from diving off of the raft, but Nicole was too freaked out and easily dodged her attempts. The other women stared uncertainly after her.

"Don't worry, just leave her," Tabitha shouted. "There's nothing we can do."

When Jerris saw the fleeing Nicole, he turned away from Brad completely and used his free hand to grab her. Then he stepped back with the girl and headed back toward the shore. Still confused and ready for a fight, Brad remained in his dinosaur form for a few moments staring after them.

When he became human again, Tabitha tossed the rope out to him, and Brad caught it. She hauled him in and he quietly climbed aboard.

"What was that all about?" asked Stacy as she sat shivering with fear and cold. "Why didn't he eat us all?"

"I'm not really sure," Brad admitted. "But in my mind, I heard a voice. It told me that if I left him the girl, he would let us go. And so I did."

"What? You mean all he wanted was one of us and you just let him have her?" Anne snapped angrily. "But that makes perfect sense, since all the sudden you're one of the things too. Or maybe you were one of those freaks all along, and you brought us here on purpose!"

"Anne, will you calm down?" Brad said irritably. "Apparently becoming a T-Rex leaves a guy with one hell of a headache. Now look, I'm going to get you off this island and back where you belong, but only if you play by my rules, got that? And first rule is, no yelling!"

"You're yelling," she pointed out.

"Okay, fine," he said more quietly. "Now everybody use some of the rope to tie yourself onto this raft. I don't think it'd be much fun to chase you down if you fall off in the middle of the Atlantic Ocean."

"Aye, aye, Captain," said Tabitha, giving Brad a little salute before she turned to help lash the two other women to the boat, then let Brad tie her on as well. "Oh, we're out of rope," she said then.

"Don't worry about me," he said. "If I can figure out how to become other animals, how hard can it be to turn into a fish as well?"

"I suppose you've got a point," she agreed. Then she sighed. "What do you suppose that guy wanted with Nicole anyway? You don't think he ate her, do you?"

"No, I don't think he did," said Brad speculatively. "If that was his only purpose, I don't think our two companions would even be alive."

"Stacy, what did Jerris want with you?" Tabitha asked. "Did he ever try anything funny?"

"If you're asking if he tried to mate with us, the answer is no," she said, shivering some more. Brad pulled a blanket from one of the packs to wrap around her shoulders. "He didn't even keep us in his cave. We were placed in the cave with all the single women, and sometimes men came to look us over. One of those men even carried Amanda off and mated her. But Jerris himself never bothered to look at any of us again. They kept telling us we'd been marked for food. It was so frightening, thinking we could die at any moment and be eaten by the very people who were keeping us alive."

"Yeah, I guess we'll never know what happens to Nicole, will we?" Brad pointed out. "I mean, once we get back home, we'll probably go back to school, finish out the term, and get on with our lives, right? Maybe we won't even see each other ever again."

"Even us?" Tabitha wanted to know. "Are you going to just forget that whole three weeks every happened between us too?"

"Is that what you want?" he asked her.

"I—don't know," she answered, her cheeks going red. "Some of it was—fun."

"Then maybe when we get back, we could try—some of it again," he replied, and the two of them shared a slow, satisfied smile.

Chapter 10

Jerris was holding the unconscious young woman in one hand and still held the cell phone and charger in the other. As he came to shore, he knew he needed to make certain both the phone and the girl were still in working order, but since the phone remained a mystery, he opted for making sure about the girl.

Letting the outsiders leave had been a really tough decision to make. He had intended to eat them all, since it was his duty, but then the male had actually shifted into a great one as well. He supposed it had been a great shock to his system, and maybe that was the reason he'd been so remiss in his duty. But he supposed it was much more than that.

Finding a patch of soft grass, he dropped everything from his claws and shifted back down to his human size. He set the phone aside and got down onto his haunches, hovering over the unconscious girl with a look of concern.

They were just beyond the beach and the wrecked ship, which he could see clearly as he glanced out to sea to watch the raft floating away. Yes, his reason had much more to do with the girl than anything else, in fact. When he had seen her fall into the water, it took him only a moment to realize that.

Unlike Stacy and Anne, this particular girl didn't know who Jerris was. She didn't know anything about his status, or his abilities, or anything he had done in the past. She hadn't witnessed his previous behavior, nor had she been party to the way he had been treating the other girls he had marked as food.

True, both Jean and Amanda knew what he was like, acting like a big bully and stomping around in all his Neanderthal glory. But now that he had transformed into a Cro-Magnon man he could easily convince those two that he was different than he'd been before. They didn't know that such a transformation was only skin deep, and any changing he would be doing beyond that would all have to come from him.

And change was exactly what he knew was needed now. Trip wanted it, and he wanted it, but mostly it was needed for the tribe. The people lacked unity, and they lacked heart. No one ever looked at each other anymore. They all just looked through each other, almost as if they were simply waiting for the end. For the day when the world shifted yet again, when another bright object filled the sky and tore everything—including their little island this time—asunder, leaving only red skies and ash in its wake.

Only the magic had saved them the last time—but then, they hadn't been what they were now. Then, they had been tiny creatures, not the great beast Jerris had learned to become. So many times they'd bathed in the spring, him and Trip. So many transformations, becoming what they needed to survive. He still remembered the day when they'd chosen strong males from among the people to drink, and the hunters had first been born.

And now, he had transformed yet again. He knew it was needed, and he also knew that Trip needed to drink as well. To drink of the magic, and reform their world, just as they'd always done before. And this girl, this smallish slip of a modern girl, she was going to help him do that. He had always carefully avoided making children before, but this time, he had every intention of breaking that rule. They needed stronger bloodlines, a new way to survive.

Vel's little girl was proof that the decision was correct. She was born with the mark, a mark of the gods which until now had been reserved only for the males. The fact that the gods had chosen Talon spoke volumes to Jerris. That was why he'd chosen to drink from the spring. That was why he'd taken the girl that now laid before him in the grass.

The girl stirred and opened her eyes, screaming as soon as she caught sight of his close proximity to her. Jerris sat back and showed her his hands, trying to look as non-threatening as possible.

She got to her feet and tried to run, but Jerris made short work of catching her and sitting her on the grass again. She clawed and scratched, and even tried to bite at his hands, which only made him laugh. She could hardly hurt one such as him with her tiny, perfect teeth.

Still, she had a lot of spunk. Something that he could admire. He believed that even if he hadn't intended to mate with her before, seeing her like this would have made him change his mind. She must have sensed that mood in him, for as he continued to hold her to his chest, he felt her heart stutter and begin to pound.

"What am I doing here?" she demanded hotly. "What happened to that creepy dinosaur who was chasing after our raft?"

"It all right now," Jerris said softly. "Dinosaur does not want to eat you."

"What? Why not?"

"Not want to ruin beautiful face," he said, stroking her hair out of her eyes.

"Stop that!" she growled. "Where did you come from anyway? God, I'm so tired of this crazy place. Nothing makes any sense at all around here."

"That because you trying to make sense out of it with wrong rules," Jerris pointed out. "This place not have same rules as others. Have to make sense using its own rules."

"And that makes even less sense," she told him. "You're him, aren't you? You're the only man here, and there's no huge, shape shifting beast trying to use me like a stick of gum. Logic must dictate that you are the missing dino."

"Not lie to you," he shrugged, hiding his amusement at her words. "I am creepy dinosaur."

"Wow, I really can't believe you can turn into something so huge," she said as she pressed on one of his arm muscles curiously. This reminded him that he still had not let go.

"If I take arms away, you not run?" he asked.

"Where would I run that you couldn't find me?" she asked with resignation.

"You been hiding all this time," he said.

"I had help," she scoffed. "I never could have done it on my own.

"At least honest," he smirked. "I would have eat you then. Now, have another idea for you. You join others helping teach. You join me in my cave at night. I have other mates, but make you top mate over them. You teach them talk, be more like you."

Nicole stared at Jerris speculatively when he said that. "I suppose if I said no you'd just eat me anyway," she sighed.

"Old Jerris would," he admitted. "Not now. Now, want to learn new way. Want you teach me, too. What name you called?"

"Nicole," she told him. "Not a very dinosaur kind of a name, but it's all I've got. I suppose you'll just have to learn to like it, eh?"

"It not bad," he said. "Sound like name Jean gave weird round thing she show at object class."

Giggling, she said, "No, no, she must have shown you a nickel. I can see why you might think that, though. They do sound a lot alike. Even more so to a caveman, I'd suppose. You know, I had expected you to be really ugly after hearing all the things those girls were saying about you. I wonder why neither of them told me you were so good-looking."

Nicole looked Jerris over speculatively. Vel had said that Jerris was one of the old ones, and she had taken that to mean that he was a Neanderthal, like Trip. He was supposedly at least as old as the shaman, but he didn't look above the age of twenty to her as she looked at him now.

"How come you don't look like Trip?" she finally asked. "I was told you're just as old as him. Was Vel mistaken?"

"Not mistaken," he shrugged. "I been alive longer than Trip by one or two turns of the moon, but can't count all the turning suns of our time. Magic rule this place, keeps us as we are. Me think Trip hopes to die since he refuses to take more magic, but I not want same."

"But how can that be?" she asked.

"Not know," he shrugged. "I drink water from spring, now not look same anymore. Found spell to transform when me and Trip very young. Been using ever since. All ancestors of hunters drank from spring, now they shift too. Spring helps us remain."

"Could you show me this spring sometime?" Nicole asked hopefully.

"Location of spring very secret," he said. "Not show to you until I know you better. When I know I can trust."

"I understand," she said, even though she was disappointed by his words.

"Come, we return to tribe now. Your friends not going to look for you again. They left as soon as I brought you to shore. We go to cave, rest and eat, then talk more. Maybe even mate once not so tired."

Nicole flushed at his words, and Jerris reached out a hand to turn her face up so he could look at her. She blushed again as he leaned down to give her a kiss.

"We could always mate now, and then go," he offered with a slight smirk.

"No, I think I actually am too tired," she admitted. "I wouldn't want to fall asleep halfway through something like that."

"Never have problem like that," he said, puffing his cheeks at her. Then he turned and picked up the cell phone and the charger with one of his hands, and started to walk towards the mountain in the distance.

Nicole followed Jerris as he headed back to the caves. At some point he reached down and took her hand to help her keep going, and finally they stepped inside.

Most of the people stopped and stared at the relative stranger, trying to work out who he was. As soon as they had an idea, though, they quickly looked away again. Nicole was also a bit of a novelty, since only the gatherers had ever seen her before this.

Trip stared pointedly at Jerris as he walked up to his hearth, sensing it was him more by his energy and attitude than by his face.

He signed, "You've been to the spring again, haven't you? I thought we agreed to avoid it until the need became great again."

"You wanted me to change," he signed back. "The old me was too stuck in the ancient ways. This new, modern me will be more willing to change. I think I'm going to do a much better job now than I ever did before."

"Nonsense," Trip scoffed. "I am still of the old people, and I'm just as willing to change."

"Maybe it's about time you changed again as well," Jerris pointed out. "You have no idea how limited the Neanderthal mind actually is. I'm willing to say that once you change, you would easily notice the difference."

"I have my reasons for waiting," Trip told him. "I wanted the old memories to pass on to the young shamans, as well you know. I am uncertain a Cro-Magnon mind can receive them, and Talon is too young now for me to try."

"There is another way you can give them," Jerris reminded him. "Pass them on to a child of your own."

"What?" he scoffed. "Who would want to mate with someone who looked like me? Don't be silly. Women have always feared to mate with me because of my great power. You know that."

"You are blind, old man," Jerris scoffed. "Anissa has always been willing if you would but look in her direction. Why do you think she took the job of guarding the women? It was so she could be near you."

"I don't believe you," he scoffed then.

"Why don't you ask her for yourself?" he replied.

"Hey, I'm very tired," Nicole mentioned after watching their movements for a while. "When can we get some rest? Old Trip here had us walking for hours and hours, and then I had to help with that raft as well. I'm really beat."

"Why are you even here?" Trip wanted to know. "Has Jerris eaten your companions?"

"No, he let them go, actually," she said. "I don't really know why."

"It was a trade, keeper," said Jerris as his hand came up to smooth down Nicole's spine, making her blush. "I get rid of old me. I change old ways. Then as I went to stop outsiders it came to me. Outsiders are not problem, they solution. I let man go so he could find way to help. Saw that you gave him gift, so sure he will return one day. But in return, I take something as well. This girl will become my new mate. She show me how to be the Jerris I want to become."

"Changing your face and changing your mate won't be enough," Trip warned him. "You've still got a long way to go."

"At least I am willing to try," said Jerris, and Trip nodded his understanding with a smile.

"Go now, Jerris," he said. "Nicole look ready to sleep on feet. If you want to be caring mate, start by showing you care."

Jerris wrapped an arm around Nicole's shoulders. Then he turned and wrapped the other beneath her knees, taking her up into his arms. He carried her gently all the way home.

*****

At the hearth later that night, Jerris brought Nicole to sit with Jean and Amanda, and he nodded shyly to the men as he sat down beside them. Both Vel and Furr seemed willing to welcome him, but Gruff held his own opinion in reserve.

"Not Neanderthal now," Jerris said with a shrug. "Not belong on that side."

"Still following the old traditions as always, I see," Jean teased him.

"No, not following this time," he explained. "I went to usual spot. Others not want me by their side because not Neanderthal. Made me go here with you."

"So now you get to see how the other half lives," Amanda smirked. "But I bet you'll find out this side of the hearth is a whole lot better in the end. Over here, you get to have friends. And none of us would throw you out just for being a bit different."

"Why you not hate me?" he asked her. "I bite you for food, but you smiling into my eyes."

"I've never been one to hold a grudge," she explained. "Besides, thanks to you I have Furr, and our new baby Ren. See, here he is now. I think he has his father's eyes."

"This place so different in so little time," said Jerris as he looked around. "Everyone in whole tribe seem more calm, more happy. On another day, you never would have look in my eye. I would have thought you want to mate if you look there. But now I see by look that your eyes are for Furr even if they see me. You talk to me just to be nice. I never think it could happen like that, but see it all through cave. Women not seem frightened anymore."

"People are making friends," Jean explained. "They are talking to each other, working together to get the work done, sharing stories and understandings. But more importantly, they each know who belongs to who. They don't misunderstand each other's intentions just because they interact. The old rules didn't really help keep people safe, they really just kept them apart. Trip told me once before that he was afraid the tribe was dying, and no matter how much I wish I could say he was wrong, in a way it is. You can see that easily enough. Nobody was communicating, nobody was planning for the future, and that's no way to live if you're hoping to thrive and grow. The only way the tribe is going to survive is for everyone to work together to save it—the women as well as the men. Can you not see this too?"

"Jean is right," Jerris agreed. "The magic to speed births didn't help. Making more babies faster not the real answer when they dying off from disease and famine just as fast. We need real medicine as well as magic. People must work together to stay alive. All of us could learn to sew, or learn to make meals, or learn to gather, or learn to hunt. You show that to us, Jean, and for that the tribe is very grateful. The tribe's protector, doubly so. We are all in Jean's debt."

Jean smiled over at Vel as he watched this exchange, and he smiled back at her, nodding his agreement. He leaned forward to take her hand in his own as he added, "I agree, Jean has saved us all. I very grateful to Jean too. She has truly given life to the people, and she did it all without even trying. She give Talon, who will be a great shaman one day; she give teachings, which have shown us value of women, and she give us hope for another day. We owe her much thanks."

Diana and Gruff were sitting just behind Jean and Vel, watching this exchange with interest. Diana leaned forward to reach Jean's ear and said, "Well, I never would have believed it if I hadn't seen it with my own two eyes, but you've actually gotten Jerris to become a team player."

"Yeah, me neither," Jean agreed.

"He actually cleans up nice," Diana chuckled, glancing over to see if Gruff was listening to them.

"Woman!" he signed. "Your eyes belong with me!"

Jean giggled at this, and then she felt a pair of strong arms slide around her as Vel pulled her against him from behind.

"And what is your thought to Jerris now?" he asked against the shell of her ear. Heat suffused her body as she leaned back against him. "Do you also think he cleans up nice?"

"What about Jerris?" she wanted to know. "I wouldn't know a thing about Jerris, my mate, since my eyes are only ever looking at you."

"Is that right?" he asked, playfully puffing his cheeks at her. "Because I swear I heard you and my mother saying other words not quite to my liking just now."

"I wasn't saying anything of the kind," she laughed. "Besides, I'm sure it was just a casual observation. There's no way your mother would want Jerris instead of Gruff, you know."

Gruff heard her laugh, and he laughed as well, which made Vel laugh to see his father giving it a try. Then, several of those around them also started in.

Suddenly, Talon made a little noise that startled both parents and grandparents alike. A few others in the vicinity also stopped to listen even though now the laughter was spreading out through the cave as more and more people joined in.

"Oh my!" Diana gasped. "Did she just—"

"I think she did," Jean agreed as they all gathered around her little bed.

Talon did it again, this time the clear, unmistakable sound of her laughter filling the air.

"It looks like your daughter won't have any problems learning to laugh," said Jean to Vel with a smug smile.

"Of course not," he agreed. "She has a really good teacher, after all."

"You guys are really making me feel loved around here tonight," Jean said with a smile.

"What is love?" Vel wanted to know.

Diana made a little sign of a circle going over her heart.

Vel smiled, and asked, "Is love the feeling in your heart you only get with your mate? It close to how Talon makes me feel, but different too?"

"Love is when you know you are wanted, and needed, and understood," said Jean. "When people like and accept you for yourself, and don't expect you to act a certain way just for them, but are happy with you just as you are. And most especially, love is a feeling right here, right in your heart, that tells you that you're right where you always want to be."

"You mean in my arms?" he smirked.

"In your heart," she told him. "Always."

"Come with me, Jean," said Vel with a smile.

"What? Why?"

"I'd like us to build more thrust," he replied.

"Don't you mean trust?" she asked as he pulled her to her feet and they started to walk away.

"No," he answered. "I mean thrust. Mother, watch Talon for a while?"

"Of course," she grinned. "Take all the time you want."

"In that case, you better watch her for the night."

The end.

If you enjoyed this ebook and want me to keep writing more, please leave a review of it on the store where you bought it. By doing so you'll allow me more time to write these books for you as they'll get more exposure. So thank you. :)

Get Free Romance eBooks!

Hi there. As a special thank you for buying this book, for a limited time I want to send you some great ebooks completely **free of charge** directly to your email! You can get it by going to this page:

www.saucyromancebooks.com/physical

You can see a the cover of these books on the next page:

These ebooks are so exclusive you can't even buy them.
When you download them I'll also send you updates when
new books like this are available.

Again, that link is:

www.saucyromancebooks.com/physical

Now, if you enjoyed the book you just read, please leave a
positive review of it where you bought it (e.g. Amazon). It'll
help get it out there a lot more and mean I can continue writing
these books for you. So thank you. :)

More Books By Jane Rowe

If you enjoyed that, you'll love The Dragon King's Baby by Mary T Williams (sample and description of what it's about below - search 'The Dragon King's Baby by Mary T Williams' on Amazon to get it now).

Description:

When her father tells Addie she is to marry the Dragon Shifter King in a marriage of convenience, she is less than pleased. Sure it will join the human and dragon communities and make things better for their people, but what about what she wants? Expected to have her new king Seathan's child fairly early on, her stubbornness doesn't want to give in.

But when she meets her husband to be, she can't help but fall for this powerful ruler.

That coupled with the pleasure he offers in the bedroom, and the new queen soon becomes pregnant as planned.

Though not everyone is happy with this new alliance, and some will stop at nothing to destroy Addie and Seathan's marriage...

Even if that means all out war!

Will the two be able to survive the new threat while falling for each other more and more each day?

Sample:

Princess Adelaide sat on the balcony that jutted out of her royal suite. She looked out over her father's kingdom, content with her life. The skyscraper in which she, her parents, the king and queen of the human kingdom, Lomena, lived was the tallest building, and her line of sight extended for miles and miles. Lomena sat safe on an island surrounded by the ocean. Addie, as she was more familiarly called, couldn't see the mainland, so large was the island. The skyscraper in which she resided with her family, a battalion of servants, and royal courtiers sat in the middle of the island and was protected by a contingent of human soldiers.

A knock sounded at her door, and Addie turned her head to call out. Her handmaid and close friend, Jeanne, entered without waiting for an answer, bustling in with a tray of food holding her breakfast.

"Good morning, Addie," Jeanne called in her sweet, high-pitched voice. She set the tray down, and as was customary for the pair, sat across from Addie to join her in her repast.

"Good morning, Jeanne. Thank you," Addie replied, handing her friend a napkin from the tray before pouring them each a cup of coffee. As she divided the food, a note on the tray caught her eye. "Who's the note from?"

Jeanne rolled her eyes. "Thomas met me in the kitchen and asked that I give this to you." Thomas was the king's second in command, sort of a vice president type figure.

"Such formality," Addie mused aloud. She put a piece of fruit in her mouth, enjoying the succulent sweetness, before she opened the note. Her eyebrow lifted. "I've been summoned to his office."

"Really?" Jeanne asked, glancing sideways at the note Addie had dropped on the tray. "How weird that he asked you like that."

Addie sighed. "He only does this when he has something to talk to me about that he knows I won't like. I can't ignore a formal summons, but I can skip dinner." They laughed together.

"Hmmm," Jeanne hummed in thought. She chewed on a hunk of cantaloupe and swallowed before saying, "I wonder what he could possibly want."

"Who knows? The last time he summoned me like this, it was to tell me that I had to go to college whether I liked it or not."

"Yeah, but you wanted to go to college, so that doesn't really count," Jeanne reminded her as she speared a piece of watermelon with her fork.

"True, even though he insisted my major be in foreign diplomacy rather than literature," Addie grumbled.

"You minored in literature and have written and published several short stories."

Addie nodded thoughtfully as she sipped her coffee. "I still wonder if they published them just because I'm the king's daughter."

"No way," Jeanne assured her. "I read them. They're really good."

"You have to say that. You're my friend," Addie returned with a grin. "Anyway, I can't imagine what he wants."

"Well, let's finish breakfast so you can choose what to wear. You might as well look your best when you go down to meet him," Jeanne commented.

Addie cut into her omelet fiercely, scraping the plate with her fork and causing both herself and Jeanne to shudder at the sound. "Sorry. You know, he could just come up here or talk to me at dinner, but no! That's why I'm kind of freaking out right now."

Jeanne waved her empty fork around. "I wouldn't worry about it until you get there."

"Yeah, I guess." Addie changed the subject. "Any gossip I need to know about?"

Jeanne giggled and launched into a ten minute discussion about one of her father's aides who had been caught dillydallying with a were, a big no-no among the humans. Addie's worries about her father's desire to meet with her melted away as she listened to the newest scandal.

*****

Addie descended alone in the elevator, dressed in the dove-gray pantsuit Jeanne had chosen for her, assuming her father had called her to his office to discuss a business matter. Addie had admired herself in the mirror after putting the suit on. Her ample bosoms and generous curves filled the suit as if it had been tailored for her, which, of course, it had been. She'd asked Jeanne to pull her hair up in a professional looking up-do and had put on minimal makeup. The soft fabric of her suit felt smooth under her hands as she ran her hands over her clothes and hair just before the elevator door opened.

She stepped into the foyer that led to her father's office. The opulence was understated, but it was there in the stainless steel and glass, the original art hanging on the walls, and the polished older woman behind the desk waiting to greet her father's guests.

"Good morning, Adelaide," the woman greeted, standing as she spoke in a show of respect for a member of the royal family. Her gray hair was perfectly coiffed, her clothes immaculate, and although she was her father's secretary, Addie knew she held a great deal of power.

"Good morning, Ginger," Addie replied, inwardly grinning at the almost silly name for such an elegant woman. "Is my father ready to see me?"

"Yes, dear," Ginger replied. She stepped around her desk to stand close to Addie. She leaned in and whispered, "Your father and Thomas are in there. I don't know what's going on, but it's big."

Addie's stomach clenched. If Ginger felt it was necessary to warn her, she was in trouble. She took Ginger's hand and squeezed it, hoping to gather some of the woman's strength. "Thank you, Ginger. I hope I'm not in trouble."

Ginger looked at her, her face pinched with concern. "I'll be here if you need me. Your mother also told me to tell you to come see her as soon as this meeting is over."

Dear gods! This must be something awful! Addie thought, but her face didn't show her worry. She'd learned from an early age to keep her thoughts from crossing her face unless she wanted them to be known. She smiled at Ginger. "Well, here goes."

Addie put her hand on the door, took a deep, calming breath meant to ease the stressful tension in her body, and pushed the door open. Her father and Thomas, his second in command, rose when she entered. She looked around the room; the men were alone. Her father, King George, never included anyone in private family business. This was something else.

"Addie, come on in," George called to her.

She realized she'd been standing at the door, thoughts in disarray, staring at her father and Thomas. She put a smile on her face and stepped in, listening to the swish of the door as it closed behind her. She felt trapped by the sound and the men's eyes as they watched her cross the plush, white rug and take a seat.

Her father had chosen to sit at the head of the conference table with Thomas on his right. He rose to kiss her cheek chastely and gestured that she sit to his left. Again she felt serious concern; he never made her sit at the table like an associate. Normally, they sat on the leather couch and comfortable chairs he had in his office. Her nerves were on fire, especially when her father grinned at her like a cat with a mouse in its sights.

"Addie, I have something very important to speak to you about this morning," George began.

"Why is Thomas here?" Addie asked abruptly. She looked at Thomas apologetically. "I'm sorry, Thomas."

"No offense, Addie," Thomas said with a small, almost uncomfortable smile. "You're not used to such formal meetings."

"No, which makes me wonder what this is about," Addie said, looking back to her father with an eyebrow raised.

"Addie, how old are you?"

Addie's eyes narrowed and she pursed her lips. Her father knew the answer to that question. "I'm twenty-seven."

"Twenty-seven. Perfect," George murmured, nodding at Thomas.

"Father, pardon my language, but what the hell is going on? You know how old I am," Addie said, glaring at her father.

George's smile broadened, and he looked absolutely delighted by her question. "I've made a wonderful arrangement for you."

"Arrangement?" The word frightened her. "What kind of arrangement?"

George took a deep breath, a sign that he wasn't expecting this to go well once he made his announcement, but he was pretending he thought she'd be happy. "You are getting married."

Silence permeated the room. Addie's breath had stopped, her pulse hammered, and she felt a little faint. After several moments, she found her voice again. "Excuse me? I don't think I heard you correctly."

George and Thomas exchanged a glance. George sat forward and reached for Addie's hand, but she pulled it away before he could touch her. Again, the men looked at each other, and George sighed heavily, his false happiness evaporating. "Addie, I've promised that you will marry the dragon king."

The king wished for the silence of earlier. Addie leapt to her feet and yelled, "Are you kidding me? The dragon king? You promised me to someone without even asking for my opinion in the matter?"

"Addie, unfortunately, your opinion holds no sway in matters of foreign policy." Addie's eyes jerked to Thomas, who cleared his throat before continuing. "An alliance with the dragon king and his kingdom is required for our safety and theirs. The best alliance is a marriage." Thomas finished his explanation by lifting his hands in a gesture filled with helpless resignation.

"An alliance?" Addie looked at her father. "Let me get this straight. Are you selling me to the dragon king so that he'll be on your side should a war break out? Am I a whore you are pimping out?"

"Adelaide!" her father bellowed, rising to his feet as well. "Do not use that language when speaking to the king!"

Addie bowed sarcastically. "My apologies, your Royal Highness. I thought I was having a conversation with my father."

George breathed in. "All right. We need to calm down." He returned to his seat and gestured for his daughter to do the same. "Please, sit down."

Addie lowered herself onto the edge of the chair, her back straight and prepared to fight against this decision. In a calmer voice filled with suppressed fury, she stated, "Father, I do not want to marry anyone, let alone a man I've never met, especially a man who is of a different species. That's never been done before."

"You're right, Addie. It's never been done before by our family or the dragon king's family. But many commoners of all species are married to a person of a different species. And even have children."

Addie's lip curled in derision. "Is that a not-so-subtle hint, Father? Am I supposed to get knocked up as soon as possible? Eager for grandchildren, are you?"

"It's the only way to solidify the alliance." Thomas spoke but did not meet her eyes.

"Well, God forbid love have anything to do with it," Addie replied sarcastically, her eyes shooting daggers at Thomas, then her father. "I will not marry. I will not bear the child of a man I do not know nor love."

George sat up. His demeanor changed to that of a king rather than the man who had thrown her into the air as a child. "Adelaide, you will marry. You will marry the dragon king, you will move to Wyvern, and you will produce an heir within the year."

"I have to move to the dragon kingdom?!? Leave behind everything I know, my family, my friends, my life! Father, this is absurd, backwards, and completely unfair!" Addie was close to tears, her voice hitching by the end of her sentence. She blinked once; the tears were gone, replace by anger once again.

George softened as he watched his daughter's display of strength. "I'm sorry, Addie, but this is the way of things when you are a member of the royal family. The wizards have wed into the were royal line and created an alliance. They are stronger than us now. We have no choice."

Addie rose. "You mean I have no choice but to submit to this absolutely preposterous marriage."

"If that's the way you choose to see it, then yes, I suppose so." Her father rose again and handed her some papers. "The wedding will take place a week from tomorrow." He ignored his daughter's gasp of indignation. "Your mother is aware of this and has already begun preparing. I suggest you join her."

"Have you met the dragon king?" Addie asked.

George would not meet her eyes. "No."

Addie was silent, her fury filling the room with each passing second. The papers in her hand were crumpled in her fury. "But I'm supposed to marry him," Addie hissed. She shook her head. "And when do I have to move?" she asked scathingly.

"The day after the wedding," George said. Addie stared at him, hatred plain on her face.

Thomas cleared his throat. Gently, he said, "Addie, the papers you're holding are a contract. I'll need you to sign that before you leave the office."

Her eyes didn't leave her father's as she said, "Of course. I'll sign my freedom away and bind myself to a man I've never laid eyes on. A man my father has never met. I'll give myself to this man who may or may not be a mean son-of-a-bitch."

Addie jerked the proffered pen out of Thomas' hand and signed the line he pointed at with a flourish. She slammed the pen on the table and lifted her eyes to her father's.

"I will never forgive you for this. And any child of mine will never visit this kingdom. I will never return to this kingdom. Next week will be the last time you will lay eyes on me."

*****

She refused to look at Ginger as she marched out of the office. She'd wanted to slam the door, but she was unable because of the stopper. She pushed the elevator button with such anger she hurt her finger. Ginger watched her but did not speak; the pain Addie felt was plain on her face and in her stance.

As soon as the elevator doors closed, she broke down, sobbing so hard her body put itself into the fetal position. She braced herself in the corner of the elevator and let the tears rack her body. She'd chosen the floor that would open into her mother's private rooms, and she was standing there, waiting for her daughter with Jeanne as well as Addie's best friend, Poppy.

"Addie," her mother gushed. She rushed into the elevator and helped her daughter back to her feet. With her arm around her, she guided her to the couch closest to the window, where her daughter had always liked to sit. "Sweetheart, I'm so sorry for the suddenness of this."

"The suddenness?" Addie sobbed, looking at her mother, her words garbled by tears. "This is positively the most appalling thing that's ever happened to me!"

"I know, baby, I know," Claire murmured, soothing her daughter's hair as her friends circled around her.

"Addie, Poppy and I get to go with you to Wyvern, so you won't be totally alone," Jeanne told her as her hand ran down her sobbing friend's arm.

Addie frowned as she looked at her friend. "That's not fair! You two have to give up your lives here to go with me?"

"We don't see it that way," Poppy explained. "We're excited to see new places and new things. We volunteered to go with you to help you."

Addie stared at her fairy friend, absorbing the comfort she always exuded. Her little body, only a couple of feet high, flitted about, her fairy wings moving so quickly they looked like a blur of pink. Her skin was flawless and stained a sweet pink, and her dress was also pink. Addie's father had rescued her from a were who planned to force her into slavery, and her loyalty to him, and to Addie, was absolute.

"Do you feel the same way, Jeanne?" Addie asked her handmaid, who held out a tissue as she sat on the couch next to her.

"All I've ever seen in my whole life is the human kingdom. I've only met a handful of other species during my very sheltered life. Going to the dragon kingdom, meeting new types of people, is incredibly exciting for me," Jeanne finished with a squeal of excitement. "And besides, I get to be with you, my closest friend in the world. I would never want you to be alone."

Addie smiled. At least her friends were going and she wouldn't be completely alone. But that didn't make the fact that she had to marry a stranger any better. "I'm so glad you two are going with me. Maybe it will help make it all better."

"That's my girl! Stay positive in a bad situation," Claire smiled, squeezing Addie's shoulders. "Now, I called the dress shop and they're sending a few dresses over in your size. In fact," she glanced at her watch, "they should be here in the next fifteen minutes."

Addie's eyes narrowed at her mother. "How long have you known about this little arrangement?"

Claire had the courtesy to look a little ashamed. "Okay, your father told me two days ago. I have no idea how long he's known."

Addie rolled her eyes. "I hope he at least put some thought into the plans he's made for my life. Without consulting me."

Claire sighed loudly and looked at the other two women in the room. "I know this is terrible right now, but lots of people have arranged marriages and have found their happiness."

"Was yours an arranged marriage?" Addie asked pointedly. She knew the answer.

"No. Your father and I chose each other."

"Exactly."

"I don't understand what you're going through, and I won't pretend to. Honestly, if I could stop this, I would."

Addie sighed in resignation. "I know, Mom. But just so you know, I don't care how this turns out. I will never forgive Father for this." She didn't share her threat to never return to Lomena, nor the threat that her child would never visit here.

Claire nodded but didn't reply. Her daughter's anger would burn hot for some time, she knew that. Her independence, her freedom had been compromised when her father had taken her choice away. Eventually, though, the anger's fire would begin to die down and turn to ash. Claire just hoped it wouldn't take a lifetime, though, like her father, Addie could be incredibly stubborn when she didn't get her way. The ding of the elevator announcing guests interrupted her thoughts.

"The dresses are here!" she exclaimed. Independent and fiery were perfect adjectives for her daughter, but a third was girly. Nothing pleased her daughter more than to try on clothes, dress up, fix her hair, and do her make up.

"How exciting!" Jeanne exclaimed as she jumped up to help the clerks who carried what looked like heavy bundles of lace, tulle, and fabric, all in white. They laid the bundles on every surface in the room.

A man, the owner of the store, sashayed in, ordering his lovely minions about. When the bundles were strewn about to his satisfaction, he turned to the four women. "Hello, hello, Queen Claire and Princess Adelaide." He took each of their hands in one of his and kissed the knuckles, bowing deeply. "I have brought the finest dresses in my shop for you to appraise."

"It looks as if you brought the entire store," Addie mumbled. Poppy poked her side and gave her a look. Addie nodded and changed her tone. "I have a specific style in mind, if you have it."

"Ah, I like a girl who knows what she wants!" Pierre exclaimed with a clap of his hands. "Let's get started!"

"While you are trying on dresses, I've got some details to attend to," Claire claimed.

Addie looked at her. "Like what?"

"Oh you know, the dinner, the guests, the reception, the ceremony, the list goes on and on when you're planning a wedding," Claire answered with a wave of her hand and a small laugh. "Would you like me to wait so you can help me? I don't want to make any decisions without you."

"The only decision I cared about has been made for me, thank you," Addie replied bitterly. "But I would like my opinion taken into account, so please stay here and work."

Claire nodded. "Of course, sweetheart. I'll have my assistant bring my laptop up here and make the calls and reservations with your help."

"Thank you," Addie said. She returned her attention to Pierre. "Ok, Pierre, let's see what you have to offer."

*

Want to read more? Then search 'The Dragon King's Baby Mary T Williams' on Amazon to get it now.

Also available: Taken By The Shark by Jane Rowe (search 'Taken By The Shark Jane Rowe' on Amazon to get it now).

You can also see other related books by myself and other top romance authors at:

www.saucyromancebooks.com/romancebooks

CPSIA information can be obtained
at www.ICGtesting.com
Printed in the USA
LVOW01s1135141215
466570LV00031B/2230/P